ONE STEP AHEAD OF DEATH

It was raining again and Smiley wished he had brought a hat. He crossed the road. The pavement was very wet and the echo of his own footsteps was crisp and startling.

He drew level with the first of the two pre-fabs which bordered Scarr's yard. A car was parked in the yard with its sidelights on. Curious, Smiley turned off the street and walked towards it. It was an old MG Saloon.

He heard a footstep behind him and stood up, half turning. He had begun to raise his arm as the blow fell.

It was a terrible blow—it seemed to split his skull in two. As he fell he could feel the warm blood running freely over his left ear. "Not again, oh Christ, not again," thought Smiley. But he hardly felt the rest—just a vision of his own body, far away, being slowly broken like rock; cracked and split into fragments, then nothing. Nothing but the warmth of his own blood as it ran over his face into the cinders, and far away the beating of the stonebreakers . . .

LE CARRÉ
CALL FOR THE DEAD

CALL FOR THE DEAD
THE HONOURABLE SCHOOLBOY
THE LOOKING GLASS WAR
A MURDER OF QUALITY
THE NAIVE AND SENTIMENTAL LOVER
SMILEY'S PEOPLE
THE SPY WHO CAME IN FROM THE COLD
TINKER, TAILOR, SOLDIER, SPY

CALL FOR THE DEAD

JOHN LE CARRÉ

BANTAM BOOKS
TORONTO · NEW YORK · LONDON · SYDNEY

CALL FOR THE DEAD

*A Bantam Book / published by arrangement with
Walker & Company*

PRINTING HISTORY
Walker & Company edition published August 1962
Bantam edition / December 1979
2nd printing . . . April 1980
3rd printing . . . December 1980
4th printing . . . October 1981
5th printing . . . September 1982
6th printing . . . March 1983
7th printing . . . December 1983

Cover Type Design by R. D. Scudellari

Bantam Books are published by Bantam Books, Inc. Its trademark, consisting of the words "Bantam Books" and the por-
trayal of a rooster, is Registered in U.S. Patent and Trademark
Office and in other countries. Marca Registrada. Bantam
Books, Inc., 666 Fifth Avenue, New York, New York 10103.

PRINTED IN THE UNITED STATES OF AMERICA

H   16 15 14 13 12 11 10 9 8 7

CALL FOR THE DEAD

I

A BRIEF HISTORY OF
GEORGE SMILEY

When Lady Ann Sercomb married George Smiley towards the end of the war she described him to her astonished Mayfair friends as breathtakingly ordinary. When she left him two years later in favour of a Cuban motor racing driver, she announced enigmatically that if she hadn't left him then, she never could have done; and Viscount Sawley made a special journey to his club to observe that the cat was out of the bag.

This remark, which enjoyed a brief season as a *mot*, can only be understood by those who knew Smiley. Short, fat and of a quiet disposition, he appeared to spend a lot of money on really bad clothes, which hung about his squat frame like a skin on a shrunken toad. Sawley, in fact, declared at the wedding that "Sercomb was mated to a bullfrog in a sou'wester." And Smiley, unaware of this description, had waddled down the aisle in search of the kiss that would turn him into a Prince.

Was he rich or poor, peasant or priest? Where had she got him from? The incongruity of the match was emphasised by Lady Ann's undoubted beauty, its mystery stimulated by the disproportion between the man and his bride. But gossip must see its characters in black and white, equip them with sins and motives easily conveyed in the shorthand of conversation. And so Smiley, without school, parents, regiment or trade, without wealth or poverty, travelled without labels in the guard's van of the social express, and soon became lost luggage, destined, when the divorce had come and gone, to remain unclaimed on the dusty shelf of yesterday's news.

When Lady Ann followed her star to Cuba, she gave some thought to Smiley. With grudging admiration she admitted to herself that if there were an only man in her life, Smiley would be he. She was gratified in retrospect that she had demonstrated this by holy matrimony.

The effect of Lady Ann's departure upon her former husband did not interest society—which indeed is unconcerned with the aftermath of sensation. Yet it would be interesting to know what Sawley and his flock might have made of Smiley's reaction; of that fleshy, bespectacled face puckered in energetic concentration as he read so deeply among the lesser German poets, the chubby wet hands clenched beneath the tumbling sleeves. But Sawley profited by the occasion with the merest of shrugs by remarking *partir c'est courir un peu,* and he appeared to be unaware that though Lady Ann just ran away, a little of George Smiley had indeed died.

That part of Smiley which survived was as incongruous to his appearance as love, or a taste for unrecognised poets: it was his profession, which was that of intelligence officer. It was a profession he enjoyed, and which mercifully provided him with colleagues equally obscure in character and origin. It also provided him with what he had once loved best in life: academic excursions into the mystery of human behaviour, disciplined by the practical application of his own deductions.

Some time in the twenties when Smiley had emerged from his unimpressive school and lumbered blinking into the murky cloisters of his unimpressive Oxford College, he had dreamed of Fellowships and a life devoted to the literary obscurities of seventeenth-century Germany. But his own tutor, who knew Smiley better,

2

guided him wisely away from the honours that would undoubtedly have been his. On a sweet July morning in 1928, a puzzled and rather pink Smiley had sat before an interviewing board of the Overseas Committee for Academic Research, an organisation of which he had unaccountably never heard. Jebedee (his tutor) had been oddly vague about the introduction: "Give these people a try, Smiley, they might have you and they pay badly enough to guarantee you decent company." But Smiley was annoyed and said so. It worried him that Jebedee, usually so precise, was so evasive. In a slight huff he agreed to postpone his reply to All Souls until he had seen Jebedee's "mysterious people."

He wasn't introduced to the Board, but he knew half of its members by sight. There was Fielding, the French mediaevalist from Cambridge, Sparke from the School of Oriental Languages, and Steed-Asprey who had been dining at High Table the night Smiley had been Jebedee's guest. He had to admit he was impressed. For Fielding to leave his rooms, let alone Cambridge, was in itself a miracle. Afterwards Smiley always thought of that interview as a fan dance; a calculated progression of disclosures, each revealing different parts of a mysterious entity. Finally Steed-Asprey, who seemed to be Chairman, removed the last veil, and the truth stood before him in all its dazzling nakedness. He was being offered a post in what, for want of a better name, Steed-Asprey blushingly described as the Secret Service.

Smiley had asked for time to think. They gave him a week. No one mentioned money.

That night he stayed in London at somewhere rather good and took himself to the theatre. He felt strangely light-headed and this worried him. He knew very well that he would accept, that he could have done so at the interview. It was only an instinctive caution, and perhaps a pardonable desire to play the coquette with Fielding, which prevented him from doing so.

Following his affirmation came training: anonymous country houses, anonymous instructors, a good deal of

3

travel and, looming ever larger, the fantastic prospect of working completely alone.

His first operational posting was relatively pleasant: a two-year appointment as "englischer Dozent" at a provincial German University: lectures on Keats and vacations in Bavarian hunting lodges with groups of earnest and solemnly promiscuous German students. Towards the end of each long vacation he brought some of them back to England, having already earmarked the likely ones and conveyed his recommendations by clandestine means to an address in Bonn; during the entire two years he had no idea of whether his recommendations had been accepted or ignored. He had no means of knowing even whether his candidates were approached. Indeed he had no means of knowing whether his messages ever reached their destination; and he had no contact with the Department while in England.

His emotions in performing this work were mixed, and irreconcilable. It intrigued him to evaluate from a detached position what he had learnt to describe as "the agent potential" of a human being; to devise minuscule tests of character and behaviour which could inform him of the qualities of a candidate. This part of him was bloodless and inhuman—Smiley in this role was the international mercenary of his trade, amoral and without motive beyond that of personal gratification.

Conversely it saddened him to witness in himself the gradual death of natural pleasure. Always withdrawn, he now found himself shrinking from the temptations of friendship and human loyalty; he guarded himself warily from spontaneous reaction. By the strength of his intellect, he forced himself to observe humanity with clinical objectivity, and because he was neither immortal nor infallible he hated and feared the falseness of his life.

But Smiley was a sentimental man and the long exile strengthened his deep love of England. He fed hungrily on memories of Oxford; its beauty, its rational ease and the mature slowness of its judgements. He dreamt of windswept autumn holidays at Hartland Quay, of long trudges over the Cornish cliffs, his face smooth and hot against the sea wind. This was his other secret life, and he grew to hate the bawdy intrusion of the new Germany, the stamping and shouting of uniformed students, the scarred, arrogant faces and their cheapjack answers. He resented, too, the way in which the Faculty had tampered with his subject—*his* beloved German literature. And there had been a night, a terrible night in the winter of 1937 when Smiley had stood at his window and watched a great bonfire in the university court: round it stood hundreds of students, their faces exultant and glistening in the dancing light. And into the pagan fire they threw books in their hundreds. He knew whose books they were: Thomas Mann, Heine, Lessing and a host of others. And Smiley, his damp hand cupped round the end of his cigarette, watching and hating, triumphed that he knew his enemy.

Nineteen thirty-nine saw him in Sweden, the accredited agent of a well-known Swiss small-arms manufacturer, his association with the firm conveniently backdated. Conveniently, too, his appearance had somehow altered, for Smiley had discovered in himself a talent for the part which went beyond the rudimentary change to his hair and the addition of a small moustache. For four years he had played the part, travelling back and forth between Switzerland, Germany and Sweden. He had never guessed it was possible to be frightened for so long. He developed a nervous irritation in his left eye which remained with him fifteen years later; the strain etched lines on his fleshy cheeks and brow. He learnt what it was never to sleep, never to relax, to feel at any time of day or night the restless beating of his own heart, to know the extremes of solitude and self-pity, the sudden unreasoning desire for a woman, for drink, for exercise, for any drug to take away the tension of his life.

Against this background he conducted his authentic commerce and his work as a spy. With the progress of

5

time the network grew, and other countries repaired their lack of foresight and preparation. In 1943 he was recalled. Within six weeks he was yearning to return, but they never let him go:

"You're finished," Steed-Asprey said: "train new men, take time off. Get married or something. Unwind."

Smiley proposed to Steed-Asprey's secretary, the Lady Ann Sercomb.

The war was over. They paid him off, and he took his beautiful wife to Oxford to devote himself to the obscurities of seventeenth-century Germany. But two years later Lady Ann was in Cuba, and the revelations of a young Russian cypher-clerk in Ottawa had created a new demand for men of Smiley's experience.

The job was new, the threat elusive and at first he enjoyed it. But younger men were coming in, perhaps with fresher minds. Smiley was no material for promotion and it dawned on him gradually that he had entered middle age without ever being young, and that he was—in the nicest possible way—on the shelf.

Things changed. Steed-Asprey was gone, fled from the new world to India, in search of another civilisation. Jebedee was dead. He had boarded a train at Lille in 1941 with his radio operator, a young Belgian, and neither had been heard of again. Fielding was wedded to a new thesis on Roland—only Maston remained, Maston the career man, the war-time recruit, the Ministers' Adviser on Intelligence; "the first man," Jebedee had said, "to play power tennis at Wimbledon." The NATO alliance, and the desperate measures contemplated by the Americans, altered the whole nature of Smiley's Service. Gone forever were the days of Steed-Asprey, when as like as not you took your orders over a glass of port in his rooms at Magdalen; the inspired amateurism of a handful of highly qualified, under-paid men had given way to the efficiency, bureaucracy and intrigue of a large Government department—effectively at the mercy of Maston, with his expensive clothes and his knighthood, his distinguished grey hair and silver coloured ties; Maston, who even remembered his secretary's birthday, whose manners were a by-word among the ladies of the registry; Maston, apologetically extending his empire and regretfully moving to even larger offices; Maston, holding smart houseparties at Henley and feeding on the successes of his subordinates.

They had brought him in during the war, the professional civil servant from an orthodox department, a man to handle paper and integrate the brilliance of his staff with the cumbersome machine of bureaucracy. It comforted the Great to deal with a man they knew, a man who could reduce any colour to grey, who knew his masters and could walk among them. And he did it so well. They liked his diffidence when he apologised for the company he kept, his insincerity when he defended the vagaries of his subordinates, his flexibility when formulating new commitments. Nor did he let go the advantages of a cloak and dagger man *malgré lui,* wearing the cloak for his masters and preserving the dagger for his servants. Ostensibly, his position was an odd one. He was not the nominal Head of Service, but the Ministers' Adviser on Intelligence, and Steed-Asprey had described him for all time as the Head Eunuch.

This was a new world for Smiley: the brilliantly lit corridors, the smart young men. He felt pedestrian and old-fashioned, homesick for the dilapidated terrace house in Knightsbridge where it had all begun. His appearance seemed to reflect this discomfort in a kind of physical recession which made him more hunched and frog-like than ever. He blinked more, and acquired the nickname of "Mole." But his débutante secretary adored him, and referred to him invariably as "My darling teddy-bear."

Smiley was now too old to go abroad. Maston had made that clear: "Anyway, my dear fellow, as like as not you're blown after all the ferreting about in the war. Better stick at home, old man, and keep the home fires burning."

7

Which goes some way to explaining why George Smiley sat in the back of a London taxi at two o'clock on the morning of Wednesday, 4th January, on his way to Cambridge Circus.

II

WE NEVER CLOSED

He felt safe in the taxi. Safe and warm. The warmth was contraband, smuggled from his bed and hoarded against the wet January night. Safe because unreal: it was his ghost that ranged the London streets and took note of their unhappy pleasure-seekers, scuttling under commissionaires' umbrellas; and of the tarts, gift-wrapped in polythene. It was his ghost, he decided, which had climbed from the well of sleep and stopped the telephone shrieking on the bedside table . . . Oxford Street . . . why was London the only capital in the world that lost its personality at night? Smiley, as he pulled his coat more closely about him, could think of nowhere, from Los Angeles to Bern, which so readily gave up its daily struggle for identity.

The cab turned into Cambridge Circus, and Smiley sat up with a jolt. He remembered why the Duty Officer had rung, and the memory woke him brutally from his dreams. The conversation came back to him word for word—a feat of recollection long ago achieved.

"Duty Officer speaking, Smiley. I have the Adviser on the line. . . ."

"Smiley; Maston speaking. You interviewed Samuel

9

Arthur Fennan at the Foreign Office on Monday, am I right?"

"Yes . . . yes I did."

"What was the case?"

"Anonymous letter alleging Party membership at Oxford. Routine interview, authorised by the Director of Security."

(Fennan *can't* have complained, thought Smiley; he knew I'd clear him. There was nothing irregular, nothing.)

"Did you go for him at all? Was it hostile, Smiley, tell me that?"

(Lord, he does sound frightened. Fennan must have put the whole Cabinet on to us.)

"No. It was a particularly friendly interview; we liked one another, I think. As a matter of fact I exceeded my brief in a way."

"How, Smiley, how?"

"Well, I more or less told him not to worry."

"You *what?*"

"I told him not to worry; he was obviously in a bit of a state, and so I told him."

"*What* did you tell him?"

"I said I had no powers and nor had the Service; but I could see no reason why we should bother him further."

"Is that all?"

Smiley paused for a second; he had never known Maston like this, never known him so dependent.

"Yes, that's all. Absolutely all." (He'll never forgive me for this. So much for the studied calm, the cream shirts and silver ties, the smart luncheons with ministers.)

"He says you cast doubts on his loyalty, that his career in the F.O. is ruined, that he is the victim of paid informers."

"He said *what?* He must have gone stark mad. He knows he's cleared. What else does he want?"

"Nothing. He's dead. Killed himself at 10.30 this evening. Left a letter to the Foreign Secretary. The police rang one of his secretaries and got permission to open the letter. Then they told us. There's going to be an enquiry. Smiley, you're sure, aren't you?"

"Sure of what?"

". . . never mind. Get round as soon as you can."

It had taken him hours to get a taxi. He rang three cab ranks and got no reply. At last the Sloane Square rank replied, and Smiley waited at his bedroom window wrapped in his overcoat until he saw the cab draw up at the door. It reminded him of the air raids in Germany, this unreal anxiety in the dead of night.

At Cambridge Circus he stopped the cab a hundred yards from the office, partly from habit and partly to clear his head in anticipation of Maston's febrile questioning.

He showed his pass to the constable on duty and made his way slowly to the lift.

The Duty Officer greeted him with relief as he emerged, and they walked together down the bright cream corridor.

"Maston's gone to see Sparrow at Scotland Yard. There's a squabble going on about which police department handles the case. Sparrow says Special Branch, Evelyn says C.I.D. and the Surrey police don't know what's hit them. Bad as a will. Come and have coffee in the D.O.'s glory hole. It's out of a bottle but it does."

Smiley was grateful it was Peter Guillam's duty that night. A polished and thoughtful man who had specialised in Satellite espionage, the kind of friendly spirit who always has a timetable and a penknife.

"Special Branch rang at twelve five. Fennan's wife went to the theatre and didn't find him till she got back alone at quarter to eleven. She eventually rang the police."

"He lived down in Surrey somewhere."

"Walliston, off the Kingston by-pass. Only just outside the Metropolitan area. When the police arrived they found a letter to the Foreign Secretary on the floor beside the body. The Superintendent rang the Chief Constable, who rang the Duty Officer at the Home Office, who rang the Resident Clerk at the Foreign Office, and eventually they got permission to open the letter. Then the fun started."

"Go on."

"The Director of Personnel at the Foreign Office rang us. He wanted the Adviser's home number. Said this was the last time Security tampered with his staff, that Fennan had been a loyal and talented officer, bla . . . bla . . . bla. . . ."

"So he was. So he was."

"Said the whole affair demonstrated conclusively that Security had got out of hand—Gestapo methods which were not even mitigated by a genuine threat . . . bla. . . .

"I gave him the Adviser's number and dialled it on the other 'phone while he went on raving. By a stroke of genius I got the F.O. off one line and Maston on the other and gave him the news. That was at 12.20. Maston was here by one o'clock in a state of advanced pregnancy—he'll have to report to the Minister tomorrow morning."

They were silent for a moment, while Guillam poured coffee essence into the cups and added boiling water from the electric kettle.

"What was he like?" he asked.

"Who? Fennan? Well, until tonight I could have told you. Now he doesn't make sense. To look at, obviously a Jew. Orthodox family, but dropped all that at Oxford and turned Marxist. Perceptive, cultured . . . a reasonable man. Soft spoken, good listener. Still educated; you know, facts galore. Whoever denounced him was right of course: he *was* in the Party."

"How old?"

"Forty-four. Looks older really." Smiley went on talking as his eyes wandered round the room. ". . . sensitive face—mop of straight dark hair undergraduate fashion, profile of a twenty year old, fine dry skin, rather chalky. Very lined too—lines going all ways, cutting the skin into squares. Very thin fingers . . .

12

compact sort of chap; self-contained unit. Takes his pleasures alone. Suffered alone too, I suppose."

They got up as Maston came in.

"Ah, Smiley. Come in." He opened the door and put out his left arm to guide Smiley through first. Maston's room contained not a single piece of government property. He had once bought a collection of nineteenth-century water colours, and some of these were hanging on the walls. The rest was off the peg, Smiley decided. Maston was off the peg too, for that matter. His suit was just too light for respectability; the string of his monocle cut across the invariable cream shirt. He wore a light grey woolen tie. A German would call him *flott* thought Smiley; chic, that's what he is—a barmaid's dream of a real gentleman.

"I've seen Sparrow. It's a clear case of suicide. The body has been removed and beyond the usual formalities the Chief Constable is taking no action. There'll be an inquest within a day or two. It has been agreed—I can't emphasise this too strongly, Smiley—that no word of our former interest in Fennan is to be passed to the Press."

"I see." (You're dangerous, Maston. You're weak and frightened. Anyone's neck before yours, I know. You're looking at me that way—measuring me for the rope.)

"Don't think I'm criticising, Smiley; after all if the Director of Security authorised the interview you have nothing to worry about."

"Except Fennan."

"Quite so. Unfortunately the Director of Security omitted to sign off your minute suggesting an interview. He authorised it verbally, no doubt?"

"Yes. I'm sure he'll confirm that."

Maston looked at Smiley again, sharp, calculating; something was beginning to stick in Smiley's throat. He knew he was being uncompromising, that Maston wanted him nearer, wanted him to conspire.

"You know Fennan's office has been in touch with me?"

"Yes."

"There will have to be an enquiry. It may not even be possible to keep the Press out. I shall certainly have to see the Home Secretary first thing tomorrow." (Frighten me and try again . . . I'm getting on . . . pension to consider . . . unemployable, too . . . but I won't share your lie, Maston.) "I must have all the facts, Smiley. I must do my duty. If there's anything you feel you should tell me about that interview, anything you haven't recorded, perhaps, tell me now and let me be the judge of its significance."

"There's nothing to add, really, to what's already on the file, and what I told you earlier tonight. It might help you to know (the 'you' was a trifle strong, perhaps)—it might help you to know that I conducted the interview in an atmosphere of exceptional informality. The allegation against Fennan was pretty thin—university membership in the '30s and vague talk of current sympathy. Half the Cabinet were in the Party in the '30s." Maston frowned. "When I got to his room in the Foreign Office it turned out to be rather public—people trotting in and out the whole time, so I suggested we should go out for a walk in the park."

"Go on."

"Well, we did. It was a sunny, cold day and rather pleasant. We watched the ducks." Maston made a gesture of impatience. "We spent about half an hour in the park—he did all the talking. He was an intelligent man, fluent and interesting. But nervous, too, not unnaturally. These people love talking about themselves, and I think he was pleased to get it off his chest. He told me the whole story—seemed quite happy to mention names—and then we went to an espresso café he knew near Millbank."

"A *what?*"

"An espresso bar. They sell a special kind of coffee for a shilling a cup. We had some."

"I see. It was under these . . . convivial circumstances that you told him the Department would recommend no action."

14

"Yes. We often do that, but we don't normally record it." Maston nodded. That was the kind of thing he understood, thought Smiley; goodness me, he really is rather contemptible. It was exciting to find Maston being as unpleasant as he had expected.

"And I may take it therefore that his suicide—and his letter, of course—come as a complete surprise to you? You find no explanation?"

"It would be remarkable if I did."

"You have no idea who denounced him?"

"No."

"He was married, you know."

"Yes."

"I wonder . . . it seems conceivable that his wife might be able to fill in some of the gaps. I hesitate to suggest it, but perhaps someone from the Department ought to see her and, so far as good feeling allows, question her on all this."

"Now?" Smiley looked at him, expressionless.

Maston was standing at his big flat desk, toying with the businessman's cutlery—paper knife, cigarette box, lighter—the whole chemistry set of official hospitality. He's showing a full inch of cream cuff, thought Smiley, and admiring his white hands.

Maston looked up, his face composed in an expression of sympathy.

"Smiley, I know how you feel, but despite this tragedy you must try to understand the position. The Minister and the Home Secretary will want the fullest possible account of this affair and it is my specific task to provide one. Particularly any information which points to Fennan's state of mind immediately after his interview with . . . with us. Perhaps he spoke to his wife about it. He's not supposed to have done but we must be realistic."

"You want *me* to go down there?"

"Someone must. There's a question of the inquest. The Home Secretary will have to decide about that of course, but at present we just haven't the facts. Time is short and you know the case, you made the background

15

enquiries. There's no time for anyone else to brief himself. If anyone goes it will have to be you, Smiley."

"When do you want me to go?"

"Apparently Mrs. Fennan is a somewhat unusual woman. Foreign. Jewish, too, I gather, suffered badly in the war, which adds to the embarrassment. She is a strong-minded woman and relatively unmoved by her husband's death. Only superficially, no doubt. But sensible and communicative. I gather from Sparrow that she is proving co-operative and would probably see you as soon as you can get there. Surrey police can warn her you're coming and you can see her first thing in the morning. I shall telephone you there later in the day."

Smiley turned to go.

"Oh—and Smiley. . . ." He felt Maston's hand on his arm and turned to look at him. Maston wore the smile normally reserved for the older ladies of the Service. "Smiley, you can count on me, you know; you can count on my support."

My God, thought Smiley; you really do work round the clock. A twenty-four hour cabaret, you are—"We Never Close." He walked out into the street.

III

ELSA FENNAN

Merridale Lane is one of those corners of Surrey where
the inhabitants wage a relentless battle against the
stigma of suburbia. Trees, fertilised and cajoled into
being in every front garden, half obscure the poky
"Character dwellings" which crouch behind them. The
rusticity of the environment is enhanced by the wooden
owls that keep guard over the names of houses, and by
crumbling dwarfs indefatigably poised over goldfish
ponds. The inhabitants of Merridale Lane do not paint
their dwarfs, suspecting this to be a suburban vice, nor,
for the same reason, do they varnish the owls; but wait
patiently for the years to endow these treasures with an
appearance of weathered antiquity, until one day even
the beams on the garage may boast of beetle and wood-
worm.

The lane is not exactly a cul-de-sac although estate
agents insist that it is; the further end from the Kingston
by-pass dwindles nervously into a gravel path, which in
turn degenerates into a sad little mud track across Merries Field—leading to another lane indistinguishable
from Merridale. Until about 1920 this path had led to
the parish church, but the church now stands on what is
virtually a traffic island adjoining the London road, and

17

the path which once led the faithful to worship provides a superfluous link between the inhabitants of Merridale Lane and Cadogan Road. The strip of open land called Merries Field has already achieved an eminence far beyond its own aspirations; it has driven a wedge deep into the District Council, between the developers and the preservers, and so effectively that on one occasion the entire machinery of local government in Walliston was brought to a standstill. A kind of natural compromise has now established itself: Merries Field is neither developed nor preserved by the three steel pylons, placed at regular intervals across it. At the centre is a cannibal hut with a thatched roof called "The War Memorial Shelter," erected in 1951 in grateful memory to the fallen of two wars, as a haven for the weary and old. No one seems to have asked what business the weary and old would have in Merries Field, but the spiders have at least found a haven in the roof, and as a sitting-out place for pylon-builders the hut was unusually comfortable.

Smiley arrived there on foot just after eight o'clock that morning, having parked his car at the police station, which was ten minutes' walk away.

It was raining heavily, driving cold rain, so cold it felt hard upon the face.

Surrey police had no further interest in the case, but Sparrow had sent down independently a Special Branch officer to remain at the police station and act if necessary as liaison between Security and the police. There was no doubt about the manner of Fennan's death. He had been shot through the temple at point blank range by a small French pistol manufactured in Lille in 1957. The pistol was found beneath the body. All the circumstances were consistent with suicide.

Number fifteen Merridale Lane was a low, Tudor-style house with the bedrooms built into the gables, and a half-timbered garage. It had an air of neglect, even disuse. It might have been occupied by artists, thought Smiley. Fennan didn't seem to fit here. Fennan was Hampstead and *au-pair* foreign girls.

18

He unlatched the gate and walked slowly up the drive to the front door, trying vainly to discern some sign of life through the leaded windows. It was very cold. He rang the bell.

Elsa Fennan opened the door.

"They rang and asked if I minded. I didn't know what to say. Please come in." A trace of a German accent.

She must have been older than Fennan. A slight, fierce woman in her fifties with hair cut very short and dyed to the colour of nicotine. Although frail, she conveyed an impression of endurance and courage, and the brown eyes that shone from her crooked little face were of an astonishing intensity. It was a worn face, racked and ravaged long ago, the face of a child grown old on starving and exhaustion, the eternal refugee face, the prison-camp face, thought Smiley.

She was holding out her hand to him—it was scrubbed and pink, bony to touch. He told her his name.

"You're the man who interviewed my husband," she said; "about loyalty." She led him into the low, dark drawing-room. There was no fire. Smiley felt suddenly sick and cheap. Loyalty to whom, to what. She didn't sound resentful. He was an oppressor, but she accepted oppression.

"I liked your husband very much. He would have been cleared."

"Cleared? Cleared of what?"

"There was a *prima facie* case for investigation—an anonymous letter—I was given the job." He paused and looked at her with real concern. "You have had a terrible loss, Mrs. Fennan . . . you must be exhausted. You can't have slept all night. . . ."

She did not respond to his sympathy: "Thank you, but I can scarcely hope to sleep today. Sleep is not a luxury I enjoy." She looked down wryly at her own tiny body; "My body and I must put up with one another twenty hours a day. We have lived longer than most people already.

"As for the terrible loss. Yes, I suppose so. But you know, Mr. Smiley, for so long I owned nothing but a toothbrush, so I'm not really used to possession, even after eight years of marriage. Besides, I have the experience to suffer with discretion."

She bobbed her head at him, indicating that he might sit, and with an oddly old-fashioned gesture she swept her skirt beneath her and sat opposite him. It was very cold in that room. Smiley wondered whether he ought to speak; he dared not look at her, but peered vaguely before him, trying desperately in his mind to penetrate the worn, travelled face of Elsa Fennan. It seemed a long time before she spoke again.

"You said you liked him. You didn't give him that impression, apparently."

"I haven't seen your husband's letter, but I have heard of its contents." Smiley's earnest, pouchy face was turned towards her now: "It simply doesn't make sense. I as good as told him he was . . . that we would recommend that the matter be taken no further."

She was motionless, waiting to hear. What could he say: "I'm sorry I killed your husband, Mrs. Fennan, but I was only doing my duty. (Duty to *whom* for God's sake?) He was in the Communist Party at Oxford twenty-four years ago; his recent promotion gave him access to highly secret information. Some busybody wrote us an anonymous letter and we had no option but to follow it up. The investigation induced a state of melancholia in your husband, and drove him to suicide." He said nothing.

"It was a game," she said suddenly, "a silly balancing trick of ideas; it had nothing to do with him or any real person. Why do you bother yourself with us? Go back to Whitehall and look for more spies on your drawing boards." She paused, showing no sign of emotion beyond the burning of her dark eyes. "It's an old illness you suffer from, Mr. Smiley," she continued, taking a cigarette from the box; "and I have seen many victims of it. The mind becomes separated from the body; it thinks without reality, rules a paper kingdom and devises without emotion the ruin of its paper victims. But sometimes the division between your world and ours is incomplete; the files grow heads and arms and legs, and that's a terrible moment, isn't it? The names have families as well as records, and human motives to explain the sad little dossiers and their make-believe sins. When that happens I am sorry for you." She paused for a moment, then continued:

"It's like the State and the People. The State is a dream too, a symbol of nothing at all, an emptiness, a mind without a body, a game played with clouds in the sky. But States make war, don't they, and imprison people? To dream in doctrines—how tidy! My husband and I have both been tidied now, haven't we?" She was looking at him steadily. Her accent was more noticeable now.

"You call yourself the State, Mr. Smiley; you have no place among real people. You dropped a bomb from the sky: don't come down here and look at the blood, or hear the scream."

She had not raised her voice, she looked above him now, and beyond.

"You seem shocked. I should be weeping, I suppose, but I've no more tears, Mr. Smiley—I'm barren; the children of my grief are dead. Thank you for coming, Mr. Smiley; you can go back, now—there's nothing you can do here."

He sat forward in his chair, his podgy hands nursing one another on his knees. He looked worried and sanctimonious, like a grocer reading the lesson. The skin of his face was white and glistened at the temples and on the upper lip. Only under his eyes was there any colour: mauve half-moons bisected by the heavy frame of his spectacles.

"Look, Mrs. Fennan; that interview was almost a formality. I think your husband enjoyed it, I think it even made him happy to get it over."

"How *can* you say that, how can you, now this. . . ."

"But I tell you it's true: why, we didn't even hold the thing in a Government office—when I got there I found

Fennan's office was a sort of right of way between two other rooms, so we walked out into the park and finished up at a café—scarcely an inquisition, you see. I even told him not to worry—I told him that. I just don't understand the letter—it doesn't . . ."

"It's not the letter, Mr. Smiley, that I'm thinking of. It's what he said to me."

"How do you mean?"

"He was deeply upset by the interview, he told me so. When he came back on Monday night he was desperate, almost incoherent. He collapsed in a chair and I persuaded him to go to bed. I gave him a sedative which lasted him half the night. He was still talking about it the next morning. It occupied his whole mind until his death."

The telephone was ringing upstairs. Smiley got up.

"Excuse me—that will be my office. Do you mind?"

"It's in the front bedroom, directly above us."

Smiley walked slowly upstairs in a state of complete bewilderment. What on earth should he say to Maston now?

He lifted the receiver, glancing mechanically at the number on the apparatus.

"Walliston 2944."

"Exchange here. Good morning. Your eight-thirty call."

"Oh—Oh yes, thank you very much."

He rang off, grateful for the temporary respite. He glanced briefly round the bedroom. It was the Fennans' own bedroom, austere but comfortable. There were two armchairs in front of the gas fire. Smiley remembered now that Elsa Fennan had been bedridden for three years after the war. It was probably a survival from those years that they still sat in the bedroom in the evenings. The alcoves on either side of the fireplace were full of books. In the furthest corner, a typewriter on a desk. There was something intimate and touching about the arrangement, and perhaps for the first time Smiley was filled with an immediate sense of the tragedy of Fennan's death. He returned to the drawing-room.

"It was for you. Your eight-thirty call from the exchange."

He was aware of a pause and glanced incuriously towards her. But she had turned away from him and was standing looking out of the window, her slender back very straight and still, her stiff, short hair dark against the morning light.

Suddenly he stared at her. Something had occurred to him which he should have realised upstairs in the bedroom, something so improbable that for a moment his brain was unable to grasp it. Mechanically he went on talking; he must get out of there, get away from the telephone and Maston's hysterical questions, get away from Elsa Fennan and her dark, restless house. Get away and think.

"I have intruded too much already, Mrs. Fennan, and I must now take your advice and return to Whitehall."

Again the cold, frail hand, the mumbled expressions of sympathy. He collected his coat from the hall and stepped out into the early sunlight. The winter sun had just appeared for a moment after the rain, and it repainted in pale, wet colours the trees and houses of Merridale Lane. The sky was still dark grey, and the world beneath it strangely luminous, giving back the sunlight it had stolen from nowhere.

He walked slowly down the gravel path, fearful of being called back.

He returned to the police station, full of disturbing thoughts. To begin with it was not Elsa Fennan who had asked the exchange for an eight-thirty call that morning.

IV

COFFEE AT THE FOUNTAIN

The C.I.D. Superintendent at Walliston was a large, genial soul who measured professional competence in years of service and saw no fault in the habit. Sparrow's Inspector Mendel on the other hand was a thin, weasel-faced gentleman who spoke very rapidly out of the corner of his mouth. Smiley secretly likened him to a gamekeeper—a man who knew his territory and disliked intruders.

"I have a message from your Department, sir. You're to ring the Adviser at once." The Superintendent indicated his telephone with an enormous hand and walked out through the open door of his office. Mendel remained. Smiley looked at him owlishly for a moment, guessing his man.

"Shut the door." Mendel moved to the door and pulled it quietly to.

"I want to make an enquiry of the Walliston telephone exchange. Who's the most likely contact?"

"Assistant Supervisor, normally. Supervisor's always in the clouds; Assistant Supervisor does the work."

"Someone at 15 Merridale Lane asked to be called by the exchange at 8.30 this morning. I want to know what time the request was made and who by. I want to know whether there's a standing request for a morning call, and if so let's have the details."

"Know the number?"

"Walliston 2944. Subscriber Samuel Fennan, I should think."

Mendel moved to the telephone and dialled 0. While he waited for a reply he said to Smiley: "You don't want anyone to know about this, do you?"

"No one. Not even you. There's probably nothing in it. If we start bleating about murder we'll . . ."

Mendel was through to the exchange, asking for the Assistant Supervisor.

"Walliston C.I.D. here, Superintendent's office. We have an enquiry . . . yes, of course . . . ring me back then . . . C.I.D. outside line, Walliston 2421."

He replaced the receiver and waited for the exchange to ring him. "Sensible girl," he muttered, without looking at Smiley. The telephone rang and he began speaking at once.

"We're investigating a burglary in Merridale Lane. Number 18. Just possible they used No. 15 as an observation point for a job on the opposite house. Have you got any way of finding out whether calls were originated or received on Walliston 2944 in the last twenty-four hours?"

There was a pause. Mendel put his hand over the mouthpiece and turned to Smiley with a very slight grin. Smiley suddenly liked him a good deal.

"She's asking the girls," said Mendel; "and she'll look at the dockets." He turned back to the telephone and began jotting down figures on the Superintendent's pad. He stiffened abruptly and leaned forward on the desk.

"Oh yes." His voice was casual, in contrast to his attitude; "I wonder when she asked for that?" Another pause . . . "19.55 hours . . . a man, eh? The girl's sure of that, is she? . . . Oh, I see, oh, well, that fixes that. Thanks very much indeed all the same. Well, at least we know where we stand . . . not at all, you've been very helpful . . . just a theory, that's all . . . have to think again, won't we? Well, thanks very much.

Very kind, keep it under your hat . . . Cheerio." He rang off, tore the page from the pad and put it in his pocket.

Smiley spoke quickly: "There's a beastly café down the road. I need some breakfast. Come and have a cup of coffee." The telephone was ringing; Smiley could almost feel Maston the other end. Mendel looked at him for a moment and seemed to understand. They left it ringing and walked quickly out of the police station towards the High Street.

The Fountain Café (Proprietor Miss Gloria Adam) was all Tudor and horse brasses and local honey at sixpence more than anywhere else. Miss Adam herself dispensed the nastiest coffee south of Manchester and spoke of her customers as "My Friends." Miss Adam did not do business with friends, but simply robbed them, which somehow added to the illusion of genteel amateurism which Miss Adam was so anxious to preserve. Her origin was obscure, but she often spoke of her late father as "The Colonel." It was rumoured among those of Miss Adam's friends who had paid particularly dearly for their friendship that the colonelcy in question had been granted by the Salvation Army.

Mendel and Smiley sat at a corner table near the fire, waiting for their order. Mendel looked at Smiley oddly: "The girl remembers the call clearly; it came right at the end of her shift—five to eight last night. A request for an 8.30 call this morning. It was made by Fennan himself—the girl is positive of that."

"How?"

"Apparently this Fennan had rung the exchange on Christmas Day and the same girl was on duty. Wanted to wish them all a Happy Christmas. She was rather bucked. They had quite a chat. She's sure it was the same voice yesterday, asking for the call. 'Very cultured gentleman,' she said."

"But it doesn't make sense. He wrote a suicide letter at 10.30. What happened between 8 and 10.30?"

Mendel picked up a battered old briefcase. It had no lock—more like a music case, thought Smiley. He took

26

from it a plain buff folder and handed it to Smiley. "Facsimile of the letter. Super said to give you a copy. They're sending the original to the F.O. and another copy straight to Marlene Dietrich."

"Who the devil's she?"

"Sorry, sir. What we call your Adviser, sir. Pretty general in the Branch, sir. Very sorry, sir."

How beautiful, thought Smiley, how absolutely beautiful. He opened the folder and looked at the fascimile. Mendel went on talking: "First suicide letter I've ever seen that was typed. First one I've seen with the time on it, for that matter. Signature looks O.K., though. Checked it at the station against a receipt he once signed for lost property. Right as rain."

The letter was typed, probably a portable. Like the anonymous denunciation; that was a portable too. This one was signed with Fennan's neat, legible signature. Beneath the printed address at the head of the page was typed the date, and beneath that the time: 10.30 P.M.:

"Dear Sir David,
    After some hesitation I have decided to take my life. I cannot spend my remaining years under a cloud of disloyalty and suspicion. I realise that my career is ruined, that I am the victim of paid informers.

                                    Yours sincerely,
                                    Samuel Fennan."

Smiley read it through several times, his mouth pursed in concentration, his eyebrows raised a little as if in surprise. Mendel was asking him something:

"How d'you get on to it?"

"On to what?"

"This early call business."

"Oh, I took the call. Thought it was for me. It wasn't—it was the exchange with this thing. Even then the penny didn't drop. I assumed it was for her, you see. Went down and told her."

"Down?"

"Yes. They keep the telephone in the bedroom. It's a sort of bed-sitter, really . . . she used to be an invalid, you know, and they've left the room as it was then, I suppose. It's like a study, one end; books, typewriter, desk and so forth."

"Typewriter?"

"Yes. A portable. I imagine he did this letter on it. But you see when I took that call I'd forgotten it couldn't possibly be Mrs. Fennan who'd asked for it."

"Why not?"

"She's an insomniac—she told me. Made a sort of joke of it. I told her to get some rest and she just said: 'My body and I must put up with one another twenty hours a day. We have lived longer than most people already.' There was more of it—something about not enjoying the luxury of sleep. So why should she want a call at 8.30?"

"Why should her husband—why should anyone? It's damn nearly lunch time. God help the Civil Service."

"Exactly. That puzzles me too. The Foreign Office admittedly starts late—ten o'clock, I think. But even then Fennan would be pushed to dress, shave, breakfast and catch the train on time if he didn't wake til 8.30. Besides, his wife could call him."

"She might have been shooting a line about not sleeping," said Mendel. "Women do, about insomnia and migraine and stuff. Makes people think they're nervous and temperamental. Cock, most of it."

Smiley shook his head: "No, she couldn't have made the call, could she? She wasn't home till 10.45. But even supposing she made a mistake about the time she got back, she couldn't have gone to the telephone without seeing her husband's body first. And you're not going to tell me that her reaction on finding her husband dead was to go upstairs and ask for an early call?"

They drank their coffee in silence for a while.

"Another thing," said Mendel.

"Yes?"

"His wife got back from the theatre at quarter to eleven, right?"

"That's what she says."

"Did she go alone?"

"No idea."

"Bet she didn't. I'll bet she *had* to tell the truth there, and timed the letter to give herself an alibi."

Smiley's mind went back to Elsa Fennan, her anger, her submission. It seemed ridiculous to talk about her in this way. No: not Elsa Fennan. No.

"Where was the body found?" Smiley asked.

"Bottom of the stairs."

"Bottom of the stairs?"

"True. Sprawled across the hall floor. Revolver underneath him."

"And the note. Where was that?"

"Beside him on the floor."

"Anything else?"

"Yes. A mug of cocoa in the drawing-room."

"I see. Fennan decides to commit suicide. He asks the exchange to ring him at 8.30. He makes himself some cocoa and puts it in the drawing-room. He goes upstairs and types his last letter. He comes down again to shoot himself, leaving the cocoa undrunk. It all hangs together nicely."

"Yes, doesn't it. Incidentally, hadn't you better ring your office?"

He looked at Mendel equivocally. "That's the end of a beautiful friendship," he said. As he walked towards the coin box beside a door marked "Private" he heard Mendel saying: "I bet you say that to all the boys." He was actually smiling as he asked for Maston's number.

Maston wanted to see him at once.

He went back to their table. Mendel was stirring another cup of coffee as if it required all his concentration. He was eating a very large bun.

Smiley stood beside him. "I've got to go back to London."

"Well, this will put the cat among the pigeons." The weasel face turned abruptly towards him; "or will it?" He spoke with the front of his mouth while the back of it continued to deal with the bun.

"If Fennan was murdered, no power on earth can prevent the Press from getting hold of the story," and to himself added: "I don't think Maston would like that. He'd prefer suicide."

"Still, we've got to face that, haven't we?"

Smiley paused, frowning earnestly. Already he could hear Maston deriding his suspicions, laughing them impatiently away. "I don't know," he said, "I really don't know."

Back to London, he thought, back to Maston's Ideal Home, back to the rat-race of blame. And back to the unreality of containing a human tragedy in a three-page report.

It was raining again, a warm incessant rain now, and in the short distance between the Fountain Café and the police station he got very wet. He took off his coat and threw it into the back of the car. It was a relief to be leaving Walliston—even for London. As he turned on to the main road he saw out of the corner of his eye the figure of Mendel stoically trudging along the pavement towards the station, his grey trilby shapeless and blackened by the rain. It hadn't occurred to Smiley that he might want a lift to London, and he felt ungracious. Mendel, untroubled by the niceties of the situation, opened the passenger door and got in.

"Bit of luck," he observed. "Hate trains. Cambridge Circus you going to? You can drop me Westminster way, can't you?"

They set off and Mendel produced a shabby green tobacco tin and rolled himself a cigarette. He directed it towards his mouth, changed his mind and offered it to Smiley, lighting it for him with an extraordinary lighter that threw a two-inch blue flame. "You look worried sick," said Mendel.

"I am."

There was a pause. Mendel said: "It's the devil you don't know that gets you."

They had driven another four or five miles when Smiley drew the car into the side of the road. He turned to Mendel.

30

"Would you mind awfully if we drove back to Walliston?"

"Good idea. Go and ask her."

He turned the car and drove slowly back into Walliston, back to Merridale Lane. He left Mendel in the car and walked down the familiar gravel path.

She opened the door and showed him into the drawing-room without a word. She was wearing the same dress, and Smiley wondered how she had passed the time since he had left her that morning.

Had she been walking about the house or sitting motionless in the drawing-room? Or upstairs in the bedroom with the leather chairs? How did she see herself in her new widowhood? Could she take it seriously yet, was she still in that secretly elevated state which immediately follows bereavement? Still looking at herself in mirrors, trying to discern the change, the horror in her own face, and weeping when she could not?

Neither of them sat down—both instinctively avoided a repetition of that morning's meeting.

"There was one thing I felt I must ask you, Mrs. Fennan. I'm very sorry to have to bother you again."

"About the call, I expect; the early morning call from the exchange."

"Yes."

"I thought that might puzzle you. An insomniac asks for an early morning call." She was trying to speak brightly.

"Yes. It did seem odd. Do you often go to the theatre?"

"Yes. Once a fortnight. I'm a member of the Weybridge Repertory Club you know. I try and go to everything they do. I have a seat reserved for me automatically on the first Tuesday of each run. My husband worked late on Tuesdays. He never came; he'd only go to classical theatre."

"But he liked Brecht, didn't he? He seemed very thrilled with the 'Berliner Ensemble' performances in London."

She looked at him for a moment, and then smiled suddenly—the first time he had seen her do so. It was

31

an enchanting smile; her whole face lit up like a child's.

Smiley had a fleeting vision of Elsa Fennan as a child—a spindly, agile tomboy like George Sand's 'Petite Fadette'—half woman, half glib, lying girl. He saw her as a wheedling *Backfisch,* fighting like a cat for herself alone, and he saw her too, starved and shrunken in prison camp, ruthless in her fight for self-preservation. It was pathetic to witness in that smile the light of her early innocence, and a steeled weapon in her fight for survival.

"I'm afraid the explanation of that call is very silly," she said. "I suffer from a terrible memory—really awful. Go shopping and forget what I've come to buy, make an appointment on the telephone and forget it the moment I replace the receiver. I ask people to stay the week-end and we are out when they arrive. Occasionally, when there is something I simply have to remember, I ring the exchange and ask for a call a few minutes before the appointed time. It's like a knot in one's handkerchief, but a knot can't ring a bell at you, can it?"

Smiley peered at her. His throat felt rather dry, and he had to swallow before he spoke.

"And what was the call for this time, Mrs. Fennan?"

Again the enchanting smile: "There you are. I completely forget."

V

MASTON AND CANDLELIGHT

As he drove slowly back towards London Smiley ceased
to be conscious of Mendel's presence.

There had been a time when the mere business of
driving a car was a relief to him; when he had found in
the unreality of a long, solitary journey a palliative to
his troubled brain, when the fatigue of several hours'
driving had allowed him to forget more sombre cares.

It was one of the subtler landmarks of middle age,
perhaps, that he could no longer thus subdue his mind.
It needed sterner measures now: he even tried on occasion to plan in his head a walk through a European
city—to record the shops and buildings he would pass,
for instance, in Bern on a walk from the Münster to the
University. But despite such energetic mental exercise,
the ghosts of time present would intrude and drive his
dreams away. It was Ann who had robbed him of his
peace, Ann who had once made the present so important and taught him the habit of reality, and when she
went there was nothing.

He could not believe that Elsa Fennan had killed her
husband. Her instinct was to defend, to hoard the treasures of her life, to build about herself the symbols of

normal existence. There was no aggression in her, no will but the will to preserve.

But who could tell? What did Hesse write? "Strange to wander in the mist, each is alone. No tree knows his neighbour. Each is alone." We know nothing of one another, nothing, Smiley mused. However closely we live together, at whatever time of day or night we sound the deepest thoughts in one another, we know nothing. How am I judging Elsa Fennan? I think I understand her suffering and her frightened lies, but what do I know of her? Nothing.

Mendel was pointing at a sign-post.

". . . That's where I live. Mitcham. Not a bad spot really. Got sick of bachelor quarters. Bought a decent little semi-detached down here. For my retirement."

"Retirement? That's a long way off."

"Yes. Three days. That's why I got this job. Nothing to it; no complications. Give it to old Mendel, he'll muck it up."

"Well, well. I expect we shall both be out of a job by Monday."

He drove Mendel to Scotland Yard and went on to Cambridge Circus.

He realised as he walked into the building that everyone knew. It was the way they looked; some shade of difference in their glance, their attitude. He made straight for Maston's room. Maston's secretary was at her desk and she looked up quickly as he entered.

"Adviser in?"

"Yes. He's expecting you. He's alone. I should knock and go in." But Maston had opened the door and was already calling him. He was wearing a black coat and pinstripe trousers. Here goes the cabaret, thought Smiley.

"I've been trying to get in touch with you. Did you not receive my message?" said Maston.

"I did, but I couldn't possibly have spoken to you."

"I don't quite follow?"

"Well, I don't believe Fennan committed suicide—I think he was murdered. I couldn't say that on the telephone."

Maston took off his spectacles and looked at Smiley in blank astonishment.

"Murdered? Why?"

"Well, Fennan wrote his letter at 10.30 last night, if we are to accept the time on his letter as correct."

"Well?"

"Well, at 7.55 he rang up the exchange and asked to be called at 8.30 the next morning."

"How on earth do you know that?"

"I was there this morning when the exchange rang. I took the call thinking it might be from the Department."

"How can you possibly say that it was Fennan who ordered the call?"

"I had enquiries made. The girl at the exchange knew Fennan's voice well; she was sure it was he, and that he rang at five to eight last night."

"Fennan and the girl knew each other, did they?"

"Good heavens no. They just exchanged pleasantries occasionally."

"And how do you conclude from this that he was murdered?"

"Well, I asked his wife about this call . . ."

"And?"

"She lied. Said she ordered it herself. She claimed to be frightfully absent-minded—she gets the exchange to ring her occasionally, like tying a knot in a handkerchief, when she has an important appointment. And another thing—just before shooting himself he made some cocoa. He never drank it."

Maston listened in silence. At last he smiled and got up.

"We seem to be at cross purposes," he said. "I send you down to discover why Fennan shot himself. You come back and say he didn't. We're not policemen, Smiley."

"No. I sometimes wonder what we are."

"Did you hear of anything that affects our position here—anything that explains his action at all? Anything to substantiate the suicide letter?"

Smiley hesitated before replying. He had seen it coming.

"Yes. I understood from Mrs. Fennan that her husband was very upset after the interview." He might as well hear the whole story. "It obsessed him, he couldn't sleep after it. She had to give him a sedative. Her account of Fennan's reaction to my interview entirely substantiates the letter." He was silent for a minute, blinking rather stupidly before him. "What I am trying to say is that I don't believe her. I don't believe Fennan wrote that letter, or that he had any intention of dying." He turned to Maston. "We simply cannot dismiss the inconsistencies. Another thing," he plunged on, "I haven't had an expert comparison made but there's a similarity between the anonymous letter and Fennan's suicide note. The type looks identical. It's ridiculous I know but there it is. We must bring the police in—give them the facts."

"Facts?" said Maston. "What facts? Suppose she did lie—she's an odd woman by all accounts, foreign, Jewish. Heaven knows the tributaries of her mind. I'm told she suffered in the war, persecuted and so forth. She may see in you the oppressor, the inquisitor. She spots you're on to something, panics and tells you the first lie that comes into her head. Does that make her a murderess?"

"Then why did Fennan make the call? Why make himself a nightcap?"

"Who can tell?" Maston's voice was richer now, more persuasive. "If you or I, Smiley, were ever driven to that dreadful point where we were determined to destroy ourselves, who can tell what our last thoughts on earth would be? And what of Fennan? He sees his career in ruins, his life has no meaning. Is it not conceivable that he should wish, in a moment of weakness or irresolution, to hear another human voice, feel again the warmth of human contact before he dies? Fanciful, sentimental, perhaps; but not improbable in a man so overwrought, so obsessed that he takes his own life."

Smiley had to give him credit—it was a good performance and he was no match for Maston when it came to this. Abruptly he felt inside himself the rising panic of frustration beyond endurance. With panic came an uncontrollable fury with this posturing sycophant, this obscene sissy with his greying hair and his reasonable smile. Panic and fury welled up in a sudden tide, flooding his breast, suffusing his whole body. His face felt hot and red, his spectacles blurred and tears sprang to his eyes, adding to his humiliation.

Maston went on, mercifully unaware: "You cannot expect me to suggest to the Home Secretary on this evidence that the police have reached a false conclusion; you know how tenuous our police liaison is. On the one hand we have your suspicions: that in short Fennan's behaviour last night was not consistent with the intent to die. His wife has apparently lied to you. Against that we have the opinion of trained detectives, who found nothing disturbing in the circumstances of death, and we have Mrs. Fennan's statement that her husband was upset by his interview. I'm sorry, Smiley, but there it is."

There was complete silence. Smiley was slowly recovering himself, and the process left him dull and inarticulate. He peered myopically before him, his pouchy, lined face still pink, his mouth slack and stupid. Maston was waiting for him to speak, but he was tired and suddenly utterly disinterested. Without a glance at Maston he got up and walked out.

He reached his own room and sat down at the desk. Mechanically he looked through his work. His in-tray contained little—some office circulars and a personal letter addressed to G. Smiley Esq., Ministry of Defence. The handwriting was unfamiliar; he opened the envelope and read the letter.

"Dear Smiley,

It is essential that I should lunch with you tomorrow at the Compleat Angler at Marlow. Please
do your best to meet me there at one o'clock.
There is something I have to tell you.

Yours,
Samuel Fennan."

The letter was handwritten and dated the previous
day, Tuesday, 3rd January. It had been postmarked in
Whitehall at 6.00 P.M.

He looked at it stodgily for several minutes, holding
it stiffly before him and inclining his head to the left.
Then he put the letter down, opened a drawer of the
desk and took out a single clean sheet of paper. He
wrote a brief letter of resignation to Maston, and attached Fennan's invitation with a pin. He pressed the
bell for a secretary, left the letter in his out-tray and
made for the lift. As usual it was stuck in the basement
with the registry's tea trolley, and after a short wait he
began walking downstairs. Halfway down he remembered that he had left his mackintosh and a few bits and
pieces in his room. Never mind, he thought, they'll send
them on.

He sat in his car in the car park, staring through the
drenched windscreen.

He didn't care, he just damn well didn't care. He was
surprised certainly. Surprised that he had so nearly lost
control. Interviews had played a great part in Smiley's
life, and he had long ago come to consider himself
proof against them all: disciplinary, scholastic, medical
and religious. His secretive nature detested the purpose
of all interviews, their oppressive intimacy, their ines-
capable reality. He remembered one deliriously happy
dinner with Ann at Quaglinos when he had described to
her the Chameleon-Armadillo system for beating the interviewer.

They had dined by candlelight; white skin and
pearls—they were drinking brandy—Ann's eyes wide
and moist, only for him; Smiley playing the lover and

38

doing it wonderfully well; Ann loving him and thrilled by their harmony.

". . . and so I learned first to be a chameleon."

"You mean you sat there burping, you rude toad?"

"No, it's a matter of colour. Chameleons change colour."

"Of course they change colour. They sit on green leaves and go green. Did you go green, toad?"

His fingers ran lightly over the tips of hers. "Listen, minx, while I explain the Smiley Chameleon-Armadillo technique for the impertinent interviewer." Her face was very close to his and she adored him with her eyes.

"The technique is based on the theory that the interviewer, loving no one so well as himself, will be attracted by his own image. You therefore assume the exact social, temperamental, political and intellectual colour of your inquisitor."

"Pompous toad. But intelligent lover."

"Silence. Sometimes this method founders against the idiocy or ill-disposition of the inquisitor. If so, become an armadillo."

"And wear linear belts, toad?"

"No, place him in a position so incongruous that you are superior to him. I was prepared for confirmation by a retired bishop. I was his whole flock, and received on one half holiday sufficient guidance for a diocese. But by contemplating the bishop's face, and imagining that under my gaze it became covered in thick fur, I maintained the ascendancy. From then on the skill grew. I could turn him into an ape, get him stuck in sash windows, send him naked to Masonic banquets, condemn him, like the serpent, to go about on his belly . . ."

"*Wicked* lover-toad."

And so it had been. But in his recent interviews with Maston the power of detachment had left him; he was getting too involved. When Maston made the first moves, Smiley had been too tired and disgusted to compete. He supposed Elsa Fennan had killed her husband, that she had some good reason and it just did not bother him any more. The problem no longer existed; suspicion, experience, perception, common sense—for Maston these were not the organs of fact. Paper was fact, Ministers were fact, Home Secretaries were hard fact. The Department did not concern itself with the vague impressions of a single officer when they conflicted with policy.

Smiley was tired, deeply, heavily tired. He drove slowly homewards. Dinner out tonight. Something rather special. It was only lunch-time now—he would spend the afternoon pursuing Olearius across the Russian continent on his Hansa voyage. Then dinner at Quaglinos, and a solitary toast to the successful murderer, to Elsa perhaps, in gratitude for ending the career of George Smiley with the life of Sam Fennan.

He remembered to collect his laundry in Sloane Street, and finally turned into Bywater Street, finding a parking space about three houses down from his own. He got out carrying the brown paper parcel of laundry, locked the car laboriously and walked all round it from habit, testing the handles. A thin rain was still falling. It annoyed him that someone had parked outside his house again. Thank goodness Mrs. Chapel had closed his bedroom window, otherwise the rain would have . . .

He was suddenly alert. Something had moved in the drawing-room. A light, a shadow, a human form; something, he was certain. Was it sight or instinct? Was it the latent skill of his own tradecraft which informed him? Some fine sense or nerve, some remote faculty of perception warned him now and he heeded the warning.

Without a moment's thought he dropped his keys back into his overcoat pocket, walked up the steps to his own front door and rang the bell.

It echoed shrilly through the house. There was a moment's silence, then came to Smiley's ears the distinct sound of footsteps approaching the door, firm and confident. A scratch of the chain, a click of the Ingersoll latch and the door was opened, swiftly, cleanly.

Smiley had never seen him before. Tall, fair, handsome, thirty-five odd. A light grey suit, white shirt and silver tie—*habillé en diplomate*. German or Swede. His left hand remained nonchalantly in his jacket pocket.

Smiley peered at him apologetically:

"Good afternoon. Is Mr. Smiley in, please?"

The door was opened to its fullest extent. A tiny pause.

"Yes. Won't you come in?"

For a fraction of a second he hesitated. "No thanks. Would you please give him this?" He handed him the parcel of laundry, walked down the steps again, to his car. He knew he was still being watched. He started the car, turned and drove into Sloane Square without a glance in the direction of his house. He found a parking space in Sloane Street, pulled in and rapidly wrote in his diary seven sets of numbers. They belonged to the seven cars parked along Bywater Street.

What should he do? Stop a policeman? Whoever he was, he was probably gone by now. Besides there were other considerations. He locked the car again and crossed the road to a telephone kiosk. He rang Scotland Yard, got through to Special Branch and asked for Inspector Mendel. But it appeared that the Inspector, having reported back to the Superintendent, had discreetly anticipated the pleasures of retirement and left for Mitcham. Smiley got his address after a good deal of prevarication, and set off once more in his car, covering three sides of a square and emerging at Albert Bridge. He had a sandwich and a large whisky at a new pub overlooking the river and a quarter of an hour later was crossing the bridge on the way to Mitcham, the rain still beating down on his inconspicuous little car. He was worried, very worried indeed.

VI

TEA AND SYMPATHY

It was still raining as he arrived. Mendel was in his garden wearing the most extraordinary hat Smiley had ever seen. It had begun life as an Anzac hat but its enormous brim hung low all the way round, so that he resembled nothing so much as a very tall mushroom. He was brooding over a tree stump, a wicked looking pick-axe poised obediently in his sinewy right hand.

He looked at Smiley sharply for a moment, then a grin slowly crossed his thin face as he extended his hand.

"Trouble," said Mendel.

"Trouble."

Smiley followed him up the path and into the house. Suburban and comfortable.

"There's no fire in the living-room—only just got back. How about a cup of tea in the kitchen?"

They went into the kitchen. Smiley was amused to notice the extreme tidiness, the almost feminine neatness of everything about him. Only the police calendar on the wall spoilt the illusion. While Mendel put a kettle on and busied himself with cups and saucers, Smiley related dispassionately what had happened in Bywater

Street. When he had finished Mendel looked at him for a long time in silence.

"But why did he ask you in?"

Smiley blinked and coloured a little. "That's what I wondered. It put me off my balance for a moment. It was lucky I had the parcel."

He took a drink of tea. "Though I don't believe he was taken in by the parcel. He may have been, but I doubt it. I doubt it very much."

"Not taken in?"

"Well, I wouldn't have been. Little man in a Ford delivering parcels of linen. Who could I have been? Besides, I asked for Smiley and then didn't want to see him—he must have thought that was pretty queer."

"But what was he after? What would he have done with you? Who did he think you were?"

"That's just the point, that's just it, you see. I think it was me he was waiting for, but of course he didn't expect me to ring the bell. I put him off balance. I think he wanted to kill me. That's why he asked me in: he recognised me but only just, probably from a photograph."

Mendel looked at him in silence for a while.

"Christ," he said.

"Suppose I'm right," Smiley continued, "all the way. Suppose Fennan *was* murdered last night and I *did* nearly follow him this morning. Well, unlike your trade, mine doesn't normally run to a murder a day."

"Meaning what?"

"I don't know. I just don't know. Perhaps before we go much further you'd check on these cars for me. They were parked in Bywater Street this morning."

"Why not do it yourself?"

Smiley looked at him, puzzled, for a second. Then it dawned on him that he hadn't mentioned his resignation.

"Sorry. I didn't tell you, did I? I resigned this morning. Just managed to get it in before I was sacked. So I'm free as air. And about as employable."

Mendel took the list of numbers from him and went into the hall to telephone. He returned a couple of minutes later.

"They'll ring back in an hour," he said. "Come on. I'll show you round the estate. Know anything about bees, do you?"

"Well, a very little, yes. I got bitten with the natural history bug at Oxford." He was going to tell Mendel how he had wrestled with Goethe's metamorphoses of plants and animals in the hope of discovering, like Faust, "what sustains the world at its inmost point." He wanted to explain why it was impossible to understand nineteenth-century Europe without a working knowledge of the naturalistic sciences, he felt earnest and full of important thoughts, and knew secretly that this was because his brain was wrestling with the day's events, that he was in a state of nervous excitement. The palms of his hands were moist.

Mendel led him out of the back door: three neat beehives stood against the low brick wall which ran along the end of the garden. Mendel spoke as they stood in the fine rain:

"Always wanted to keep them, see what it's all about. Been reading it all up—frightens me stiff, I can tell you. Odd little beggars." He nodded a couple of times in support of this statement, and Smiley looked at him again with interest. His face was thin but muscular, its expression entirely uncommunicative; his iron grey hair was cut very short and spiky. He seemed quite indifferent to the weather, and the weather to him. Smiley knew exactly the life that lay behind Mendel, had seen in policemen all over the world the same leathery skin, the same reserves of patience, bitterness and anger. He could guess the long, fruitless hours of surveillance in every kind of weather, waiting for someone who might never come . . . or come and go too quickly. And he knew how much Mendel and the rest of them were at the mercy of personalities—capricious and bullying, nervous and changeful, occasionally wise and sympathetic. He knew how intelligent men could be broken by

44

the stupidity of their superiors, how weeks of patient work night and day could be cast aside by such a man.

Mendel led him up the precarious path laid with broken stone to the beehives and, still oblivious of the rain, began taking one to pieces, demonstrating and explaining. He spoke in jerks, with quite long pauses between phrases, indicating precisely and slowly with his slim fingers.

At last they went indoors again, and Mendel showed him the two downstairs rooms. The drawing-room was all flowers: flowered curtains and carpet, flowered covers on the furniture. In a small cabinet in one corner were some Toby jugs and a pair of very handsome pistols beside a cup for target shooting.

Smiley followed him upstairs. There was a smell of paraffin from the stove on the landing, and a surly bubbling from the cistern in the lavatory.

Mendel showed him his own bedroom.

"Bridal chamber. Bought the bed at a sale for a quid. Box spring mattress. Amazing what you can pick up. Carpets are ex-Queen Elizabeth. They change them every year. Bought them at a store in Watford."

Smiley stood in the doorway, somehow rather embarrassed. Mendel turned back and passed him to open the other bedroom door.

"And that's your room. If you want it." He turned to Smiley. "I wouldn't stay at your place tonight if I were you. You never know, do you? Besides, you'll sleep better here. Air's better."

Smiley began to protest.

"Up to you. You do what you like." Mendel grew surly and embarrassed. "Don't understand your job, to be honest, any more than you know police work. You do what you like. From what I've seen of you, you can look after yourself."

They went downstairs again. Mendel had lit the gas fire in the drawing-room.

"Well, at least you must let me give you dinner tonight," said Smiley.

45

The telephone rang in the hall. It was Mendel's secretary about the car numbers.

Mendel came back. He handed Smiley a list of seven names and addresses. Four of the seven could be discounted; the registered addresses were in Bywater Street. Three remained: a hired car from the firm of Adam Scarr and Sons of Battersea, a trade van belonging to the Severn Tile Company, Eastbourne; and the third was listed specially as the property of the Panamanian Ambassador.

"I've got a man on the Panamanian job now. There'll be no difficulty there—they've only got three cars on the Embassy strength.

"Battersea's not far," Mendel continued. "We could pop over there together. In your car."

"By all means, by all means," Smiley said quickly; "and we can go in to Kensington for dinner. I'll book a table at the 'Entrechat'."

It was four o'clock. They sat for a while talking in a rather desultory way about bees and house-keeping, Mendel quite at ease and Smiley still bothered and awkward, trying to find a way of talking, trying not to be clever. He could guess what Ann would have said about Mendel. She would have loved him, made a person of him, had a special voice and face for imitating him, would have made a story of him until he fitted into their lives and wasn't a mystery any more: "Darling, who'd have thought he could be so *cosy!* The last man I'd ever thought would tell me where to buy cheap fish. And what a darling little house—*no bother*—he must know Toby jugs are hell and he just doesn't care. I think he's a pet. Toad, do ask him to dinner. You must. Not to giggle at but to *like*." He wouldn't have asked him, of course, but Ann would be content—she'd found a way to like him. And having done so, forgotten him.

That was what Smiley wanted, really—a way to like Mendel. He was not as quick as Ann at finding one. But Ann was Ann—she practically murdered an Etonian nephew once for drinking claret with fish, but if Mendel had lit a pipe over her *crêpe suzette*, she probably would not have noticed.

Mendel made more tea and they drank it. At about a quarter past five they set off for Battersea in Smiley's car. On the way Mendel bought an evening paper. He read it with difficulty, catching the light from the street lamps. After a few minutes he spoke with sudden venom:

"Krauts. *Bloody* Krauts. God, I hate them!"

"Krauts?"

"Krauts. Huns, Jerries. Bloody Germans. Wouldn't give you sixpence for the lot of them. Carnivorous ruddy sheep. Kicking Jews about again. Us all over. Knock 'em down, set 'em up. Forgive and forget. *Why* bloody well forget, I'd like to know? Why forget theft, murder and rape just because millions committed it? Christ, one poor little sod of a bank clerk pinches ten bob and the whole of the Metropolitan's on to him. But Krupp and all that mob—oh no. Christ, if I was a Jew in Germany I'd . . ."

Smiley was suddenly wide awake: "What would you do? What would you do, Mendel?"

"Oh, I suppose I'd sit down under it. It's statistics now, politics. It isn't sense to give them H-bombs so it's politics. And there's the Yanks—millions of ruddy Jews in America. What do they do? Damn all: give the Krauts more bombs. All chums together—blow each other up."

Mendel was trembling with rage, and Smiley was silent for a while, thinking of Elsa Fennan.

"What's the answer?" he asked, just for something to say.

"Christ knows," said Mendel savagely.

They turned into Battersea Bridge Road and drew up beside a constable standing on the pavement. Mendel showed his Police card.

"Scarr's garage? Well it isn't hardly a garage, sir, just a yard. Scrap metal he handles mostly, and second-hand cars. If they won't do for one they'll do for the other, that's what Adam says. You want to go down Prince of Wales Drive till you come to the hospital. It's tucked in there between a couple of pre-fabs. Bomb site it is really. Old Adam straightened it out with some cinders and no one's ever moved him."

"You seem to know a lot about him," said Mendel.

"I should do, I've run him in a few times. There's not much in the book that Adam hasn't been up to. He's one of our hardy perennials, Scarr is."

"Well, well. Anything on him at present?"

"Couldn't say, sir. But you can have him any time for illegal betting. And Adam's practically under the Act already."

They drove towards Battersea Hospital. The park on their right looked black and hostile behind the street lamps.

"What's under the Act?" asked Smiley.

"Oh, he's only joking. It means your record's so long you're eligible for Preventive Detention—years of it. He sounds like my type," Mendel continued. "Leave him to me."

They found the yard as the constable had described, between two dilapidated pre-fabs in an uncertain row of hutments erected on the bomb site. Rubble, clinker and refuse lay everywhere. Bits of asbestos, timber and old iron, presumably acquired by Mr. Scarr for resale or adaptation, were piled in a corner, dimly lit by the pale glow which came from the farther pre-fab. The two men looked round them in silence for a moment. Then Mendel shrugged, put two fingers in his mouth and whistled shrilly.

"Scarr!" he called. Silence. The outside light on the far pre-fab went on, and three or four pre-war cars in various stages of dilapidation became dimly discernible.

The door opened slowly and a girl of about twelve stood on the threshold.

"Your dad in, dear?" asked Mendel.

"Nope. Gone to the Prod, I 'spect."

"Righto, dear. Thanks."

They walked back to the road.

"What on earth's the Prod, or daren't I ask?" said Smiley.

"Prodigal's Calf. Pub round the corner. We can walk it—only a hundred yards. Leave the car here."

It was only just after opening time. The public bar was empty, and as they waited for the landlord to appear the door swung open and a very fat man in a black suit came in. He walked straight to the bar and hammered on it with a half-crown.

"Wilf," he shouted; "Take your finger out, you got customers, you lucky boy." He turned to Smiley; "Good evening, friend."

From the rear of the pub a voice replied: "Tell 'em to leave their money on the counter and come back later."

The fat man looked at Mendel and Smiley blankly for a moment, then suddenly let out a peal of laughter: "Not them, Wilf—they're busies!" The joke appealed to him so much that he was finally compelled to sit on the bench that ran along the side of the room, with his hands on his knees, his huge shoulders heaving with laughter, the tears running down his cheeks. Occasionally he said, "Oh dear, oh dear," as he caught his breath before another outburst.

Smiley looked at him with interest. He wore a very dirty stiff white collar with rounded edges, a flowered red tie carefully pinned outside the black waistcoat, army boots and a shiny black suit, very threadbare and without a vestige of a crease in the trousers. His shirt cuffs were black with sweat, grime and motor oil and held in place by paper-clips twisted into a knot.

The landlord appeared and took their orders. The stranger bought a large whisky and ginger wine and took it at once to the saloon bar, where there was a coal fire. The landlord watched with disapproval.

"That's him all over, mean sod. Won't pay saloon prices, but likes the fire."

"Who is he?" asked Mendel.

"Him? Scarr his name is. Adam Scarr. Christ knows why Adam. See him in the Garden of Eden: bloody grotesque, that's what it is. They say round here that if Eve gave him an apple he'd eat the ruddy core." The landlord sucked his teeth and shook his head. Then he shouted to Scarr: "Still, you're good for business, aren't you, Adam? They come bloody miles to see you, don't they? Teenage monster from outer space, that's what you are. Come and see. Adam Scarr: one look and you'll sign the pledge."

More hilarious laughter. Mendel leant over to Smiley. "You go and wait in the car—you're better out of this. Got a fiver?"

Smiley gave him five pounds from his wallet, nodded his agreement and walked out. He could imagine nothing more frightful than dealing with Scarr.

"You Scarr?" said Mendel.

"Friend, you are correct."

"TRX 0891. That your car?"

Mr. Scarr frowned at his whisky and ginger. The question seemed to sadden him.

"Well?" said Mendel.

"She was, squire, she was."

"What the hell do you mean?"

Scarr raised his right hand a few inches then let it gently fall. "Dark waters, squire, murky waters."

"Listen, I've got bigger fish to fry than ever you dreamed of. I'm not made of glass, see? I couldn't care bloody less about your racket. Where's that car?"

Scarr appeared to consider this speech on its merits. "I see the light, friend. You wish for information."

"Of course I bloody well do."

"These are hard times, squire. The cost of living, dear boy, is a rising star. Information is an item, a saleable item, is it not?"

"You tell me who hired that car and you won't starve."

"I don't starve now, friend. I want to eat better."

"A fiver."

Scarr finished his drink and replaced his glass noisily on the table. Mendel got up and bought him another.

"It was pinched," said Scarr. "I had it a few years for self-drive, see. For the deepo."

"The *what?*"

"The deepo—the deposit. Bloke wants a car for a day. You take twenty quid deposit in notes, right? When he comes back he owes you forty bob, see? You give him a cheque for thirty-eight quid, show it on your books as a loss and the job's worth a tenner. Got it?"

Mendel nodded.

"Well, three weeks ago a bloke come in. Tall Scotsman. Well-to-do, he was. Carried a stick. He paid the deepo, took the car and I never see him nor the car again. Robbery."

"Why not report it to the police?"

Scarr paused and drank from his glass. He looked at Mendel sadly.

"Many factors would argue against, squire."

"Meaning you'd pinched it yourself?"

Scarr looked shocked. "I have since heard distressing rumours about the party from which I obtained the vehicle. I will say no more," he added piously.

"When you rented him the car he filled in forms, didn't he? Insurance, receipt and so on? Where are they?"

"False, all false. He gave me an address in Ealing. I went there and it didn't exist. I have no doubt the name was also fictitious."

Mendel screwed the money into a roll in his pocket, and handed it across the table to Scarr. Scarr unfolded it and, quite unselfconscious, counted it in full view of anyone who cared to look.

"I know where to find you," said Mendel; "and I know a few things about you. If that's a load of cock you've sold me I'll break your bloody neck."

It was raining again and Smiley wished he had brought a hat. He crossed the road, entered the side street which accommodated Mr. Scarr's establishment and walked towards the car. There was no one in the street, and it was oddly quiet. Two hundred yards down the road Battersea General Hospital, small and neat, shed multiple beams of light from its uncurtained windows. The pavement was very wet and the echo of his own footsteps was crisp and startling.

He drew level with the first of the two pre-fabs which bordered Scarr's yard. A car was parked in the yard with its sidelights on. Curious, Smiley turned off the street and walked towards it. It was an old MG Saloon, green probably, or that brown they went in for before the war. The number-plate was barely lit, and caked in mud. He stooped to read it, tracing the letters with his forefinger: TRX 0891. Of course—that was one of the numbers he had written down this morning.

He heard a footstep behind him and stood up, half turning. He had begun to raise his arm as the blow fell.

It was a terrible blow—it seemed to split his skull in two. As he fell he could feel the warm blood running freely over his left ear. "Not again, oh Christ, not again," thought Smiley. But he hardly felt the rest—just a vision of his own body, far away, being slowly broken like rock; cracked and split into fragments, then nothing. Nothing but the warmth of his own blood as it ran over his face into the cinders, and far away the beating of the stonebreakers. But not here. Far away.

VII

MR. SCARR'S STORY

Mendel looked at him and wondered whether he was dead. He emptied the pockets of his own overcoat and laid it gently over Smiley's shoulders, then he ran, ran like a madman towards the hospital, crashed through the swing-doors of the out-patients' department into the bright, twenty-four hour interior of the hospital. A young coloured doctor was on duty. Mendel showed him his card, shouted something to him, took him by the arm, tried to lead him down the road. The doctor smiled patiently, shook his head and telephoned for an ambulance.

Mendel ran back down the road and waited. A few minutes later the ambulance arrived and skilful men gathered Smiley up and took him away.

"Bury him," thought Mendel; "I'll make the bastard pay."

He stood there for a moment, staring down at the wet patch of mud and cinders where Smiley had fallen; the red glow of the car's rear lights showed him nothing. The ground had been hopelessly churned by the feet of the ambulance men and a few inhabitants from the prefabs who had come and gone like shadowy vultures. Trouble was about. They didn't like trouble.

"Bastard," Mendel hissed, and walked slowly back towards the pub.

The saloon bar was filling up. Scarr was ordering another drink. Mendel took him by the arm. Scarr turned and said:

"Hello, friend, back again. Have a little of what killed Auntie."

"Shut up," said Mendel; "I want another word with you. Come outside."

Mr. Scarr shook his head and sucked his teeth sympathetically.

"Can't be done, friend, can't be done. Company." He indicated with his head an eighteen-year-old blonde with off-white lipstick and an improbable bosom, who sat quite motionless at a corner table. Her painted eyes had a permanently startled look.

"Listen," whispered Mendel; "in just two seconds I'll tear your bloody ears off, you lying sod."

Scarr consigned his drinks to the care of the landlord and made a slow, dignified exit. He didn't look at the girl.

Mendel led him across the street towards the prefabs. The side lights of Smiley's car shone towards them eighty yards down the road.

They turned into the yard. The MG was still there. Mendel had Scarr firmly by the arm, ready if necessary to force the forearm back and upwards, breaking or dislocating the shoulder joint.

"Well, well," cried Scarr with apparent delight; "She's returned to the bosom of her ancestors."

"Stolen, was it?" said Mendel. "Stolen by a tall Scotsman with a walking stick and an address in Ealing. Decent of him to bring it back, wasn't it. Friendly gesture, after all this time. You've mistaken your bloody market, Scarr." Mendel wàs shaking with anger. "And why are the side lights on? Open the door."

Scarr turned to Mendel in the dark, his free hand slapping his pockets in search of keys. He extracted a bunch of three or four, felt through them and finally unlocked the car door. Mendel got in, found the passen-

ger light in the roof and switched it on. He began me-
thodically to search the inside of the car. Scarr stood
outside and waited.

He searched quickly but thoroughly. Glove tray,
seats, floor, rear window-ledge: nothing. He slipped his
hand inside the map pocket on the passenger door, and
drew out a map and an envelope. The envelope was
long and flat, grey-blue in colour with a linen finish.
Continental, thought Mendel. There was no writing on
it. He tore it open. There were ten used five-pound
notes inside and a piece of plain postcard. Mendel held
it to the light and read the message printed on it with a
ball-point pen:

"FINISHED NOW. SELL IT."

There was no signature.

He got out of the car, and seized Scarr by the elbows.
Scarr stepped back quickly. "What's your problem,
friend?" he asked.

Mendel spoke softly. "It's not my problem, Scarr, it's
yours. The biggest bloody problem you ever had. Conspiracy to murder, attempted murder, offences under
the Official Secrets Act. And you can add to that con-
travention of the Road Traffic Act, conspiracy to de-
fraud the Inland Revenue and about fifteen other
charges that will occur to me while you nurse your
problem on a cell bed."

"Just a minute, copper, let's not go over the moon.
What's the story? Who the hell's talking about murder?"

"Listen, Scarr, you're a little man, come in on the
fringe of the big spenders, aren't you. Well now you're
the big spender. I reckon it'll cost you fifteen years."

"Look, shut up, will you."

"No I won't, little man. You're caught between two
big ones, see, and you're the mug. And what will I do?
I'll bloody well laugh myself sick while you rot in the
Scrubs and contemplate your fat belly. See that hospital,
do you? There's a bloke dying there, murdered by your
tall Scotsman. They found him half an hour ago bleed-

ing like a pig in your yard. There's another one dead in Surrey, and for all I know there's one in every bloody home county. So it's your problem, you poor sod, not mine. Another thing—you're the only one who knows who he is, aren't you? He might want to tidy that up a bit, mightn't he?"

Scarr walked slowly round to the other side of the car. "Get in, copper," he said.

Mendel sat in the driving seat and unlocked the passenger door from the inside. Scarr sat himself beside him. They didn't put the light on.

"I'm in a nice way of business round here," said Scarr quietly, "and the pickings is small but regular. Or was till this bloke come along."

"What bloke?"

"Bit by bit, copper, don't rush me. That was four years ago. I didn't believe in Father Christmas till I met him. Dutch, he said he was, in the diamond business. I'm not pretending I thought he was straight, see, because you're not barmy and nor am I. I never asked what he done and he never told me, but I guessed it was smuggling. Money to burn he had, came off him like leaves in autumn. 'Scarr,' he said; 'you're a man of business. I don't like publicity, never did and I hears we're birds of a feather. I want a car. Not to keep, but to borrow.' He didn't put it quite like that because of the lingo, but that's the sense of it. 'What's your proposition?' I says. 'Let's have a proposition.'

" 'Well,' he says; 'I'm shy. I want a car that no one can ever get on to, supposing I had an accident. Buy a car for me, Scarr, a nice old car with something under the bonnet. Buy it in your own name,' he says, 'and keep it wrapped up for me. There's five hundred quid for a start, and twenty quid a month for garaging. And there's a bonus, Scarr, for every day I take it out. But I'm shy, see, and you don't know me. That's what the money's for,' he says. 'It's for not knowing me.'

"I'll never forget that day. Raining cats and dogs it was, and me bent over an old taxi I'd got off a bloke in Wandsworth. I owed a bookie forty quid, and the coppers were sensitive about a car I'd bought on the never never and flogged in Clapham."

Mr. Scarr drew breath, and let it out again with an air of comic resignation.

"And there he was, standing over me like my own conscience, showering old singles on me like used tote tickets."

"What did he look like?" asked Mendel.

"Quite young he was. Tall, fair chap. But cool—cool as charity. I never saw him after that day. He sent me letters posted in London and typed on plain paper. Just 'Be ready Monday night,' 'Be ready Thursday night,' and so on. We had it all arranged. I left the car out in the yard, full of petrol and teed up. He never said when he'd be back. Just ran it in about closing time or later, leaving the lights on and the doors locked. He'd put a couple of quid in the map pocket for each day he'd been away."

"What happened if anything went wrong, if you got pinched for something else?"

"We had a telephone number. He told me to ring and ask for a name."

"What name?"

"He told me to choose one. I chose Blondie. He didn't think that was very funny but we stuck to it. Primrose 0098."

"Did you ever use it?"

"Yes, a couple of years ago I took a bint to Margate for ten days. I thought I'd better let him know. A girl answered the 'phone—Dutch too, by the sound of her. She said Blondie was in Holland, and she'd take a message. But after that I didn't bother."

"Why not?"

"I began to notice, see. He came regular once a fortnight, the first and third Tuesdays except January and February. This was the first January he come. He brought the car back Thursday usually. Odd him coming back tonight. But this is the end of him, isn't it?" Scarr held in his enormous hand the piece of postcard he had taken from Mendel.

57

"Did he miss at all? Away long periods?"

"Winters he kept away more. January he never come, nor February. Like I said."

Mendel still had the £50 in his hand. He tossed them into Scarr's lap.

"Don't think you're lucky. I wouldn't be in your shoes for ten times that lot. I'll be back."

Mr. Scarr seemed worried.

"I wouldn't have peached," he said; "but I don't want to be mixed up in nothing, see. Not if the old country's going to suffer, eh, squire?"

"Oh, shut up," said Mendel. He was tired. He took the postcard back, got out of the car and walked away towards the hospital.

There was no news at the hospital. Smiley was still unconscious. The C.I.D. had been informed. Mendel would do better to leave his name and address and go home. The hospital would telephone as soon as they had any news. After a good deal of argument Mendel obtained from the sister the key to Smiley's car.

Mitcham, he decided, was a lousy place to live.

VIII

REFLECTIONS
IN A HOSPITAL WARD

He hated the bed as a drowning man hates the sea. He hated the sheets that imprisoned him so that he could move neither hand nor foot.

And he hated the room because it frightened him. There was a trolley by the door with instruments on it, scissors, bandages and bottles, strange objects that carried the terror of the unknown, swathed in white linen for the last Communion. There were jugs, tall ones half covered with napkins, standing like white eagles waiting to tear at his entrails, little glass ones with rubber tubing coiled inside them like snakes. He hated everything, and he was afraid. He was hot and the sweat ran off him, he was cold and the sweat held him, trickling over his ribs like cold blood. Night and day alternated without recognition from Smiley. He fought a relentless battle against sleep, for when he closed his eyes they seemed to turn inwards on the chaos of his brain; and when sometimes by sheer weight his eyelids drew themselves together he would summon all his strength to tear them apart and stare again at the pale light wavering somewhere above him.

Then came a blessed day when someone must have

59

drawn the blinds and let in the grey winter light. He heard the sound of traffic outside and knew at last that he would live.

So the problem of dying once more became an academic one—a debt he would postpone until he was rich and could pay in his own way. It was a luxurious feeling, almost of purity. His mind was wonderfully lucid, ranging like Prometheus over his whole world; where had he heard that: "the mind becomes separated from the body, rules a paper kingdom . . ."? He was bored by the light above him, and wished there was more to look at. He was bored by the grapes, the smell of honeycomb and flowers, the chocolates. He wanted books, and literary journals; how could he keep up with his reading if they gave him no books? There was so little research done on his period as it was, so little creative criticism on the seventeenth century.

It was three weeks before Mendel was allowed to see him. He walked in holding a new hat and carrying a book about bees. He put his hat on the end of the bed and the book on the bedside table. He was grinning.

"I bought you a book," he said; "about bees. They're clever little beggars. Might interest you."

He sat on the edge of the bed. "I got a new hat. Daft really. Celebrate my retirement."

"Oh yes, I forgot. You're on the shelf too." They both laughed, and were silent again.

Smiley blinked. "I'm afraid you're not very distinct at the moment. I'm not allowed to wear my old glasses. They're getting me some new ones." He paused. "You don't know who did this to me, do you?"

"May do. Depends. Got a lead, I think. I don't know enough, that's the trouble. About your job, I mean. Does the East German Steel Mission mean anything to you?"

"Yes, I think so. It came here four years ago to try and get a foot in the Board of Trade."

Mendel gave an account of his transactions with Mr. Scarr. ". . . Said he was Dutch. The only way Scarr had of getting in touch with him was by ringing a Prim-

rose telephone number. I checked the subscriber. Listed
as the East German Steel Mission, in Belsize Park. I
sent a bloke to sniff round. They've cleared out. Nothing there at all, no furniture, nothing. Just the telephone, and that's been ripped out of its socket."

"When did they go?"

"3rd January. Same day as Fennan was murdered."
He looked at Smiley quizzically. Smiley thought for a
minute and said:

"Get hold of Peter Guillam at the Ministry of Defence
and bring him here tomorrow. By the scruff of the
neck."

Mendel picked up his hat and walked to the door.

"Goodbye," said Smiley; "thank you for the book."

"See you tomorrow," said Mendel, and left.

Smiley lay back in bed. His head was aching. Damn,
he thought, I never thanked him for the honey. It had
come from Fortnums, too.

Why the early morning call? That was what puzzled
him more than anything. It was silly, really, Smiley supposed, but of all the unaccountables in the case, that
worried him most.

Elsa Fennan's explanation had been so stupid, so no-
ticeably unlikely. Ann, yes; she would make the exchange stand on its head if she'd felt like it, but not Elsa
Fennan. There was nothing in that alert, intelligent little
face, nothing in her total independence to support the
ludicrous claim to absent-mindedness. She could have
said the exchange had made a mistake, had called the
wrong day, anything. Fennan, yes; he had been absent-
minded. It was one of the odd inconsistencies about
Fennan's character which had emerged in the enquiries
before the interview. A voracious reader of Westerns
and a passionate chess player, a musician and a spare
time philosopher, a deep thinking man—but absent-
minded. There had been a frightful row once about him
taking some secret papers out of the Foreign Office,
and it turned out that he had put them in his despatch

case with his *Times* and the evening paper before going home to Walliston.

Had Elsa Fennan, in her panic, taken upon herself the mantle of her husband? Or the *motive* of her husband? Had Fennan asked for the call to remind *him* of something, and had Elsa borrowed the motive? Then what did Fennan need to be reminded of—and what did his wife so strenuously wish to conceal?

Samuel Fennan. The new world and the old met in him. The eternal Jew, cultured, cosmopolitan, self-determinate, industrious and perceptive: to Smiley, immensely attractive. The child of his century; persecuted, like Elsa, and driven from his adopted Germany to University in England. By the sheer weight of his ability he had pushed aside disadvantage and prejudice, finally to enter the Foreign Office. It had been a remarkable achievement, owed to nothing but his own brilliance. And if he was a little conceited, a little disinclined to bide the decision of minds more pedestrian than his own, who could blame him? There had been some embarrassment when Fennan pronounced himself in favour of a divided Germany, but it had all blown over, he had been transferred to an Asian desk and the affair was forgotten. For the rest, he had been generous to a fault, and popular both in Whitehall and in Surrey, where he devoted several hours each week-end to charity work. His great love was skiing. Every year he took all his leave at once and spent six weeks in Switzerland or Austria. He had visited Germany only once, Smiley remembered—with his wife about four years ago.

It had been natural enough that Fennan should join the Left at Oxford. It was the great honeymoon period of University communism, and its causes, heaven knows, lay close enough to his heart. The rise of Fascism in Germany and Italy, the Japanese invasion of Manchuria, the Franco rebellion in Spain, the slump in America and above all the wave of anti-Semitism that was sweeping across Europe: it was inevitable that Fennan should seek an outlet for his anger and revulsion. Besides, the Party was respectable then; the failure of the Labour Party and the Coalition Government had convinced many intellectuals that the Communists alone could provide an effective alternative to Capitalism and Fascism. There was the excitement, an air of conspiracy and comradeship which must have appealed to the flamboyance in Fennan's character and given him comfort in his loneliness. There was talk of going to Spain; some *had* gone, like Cornford from Cambridge, never to return.

Smiley could imagine Fennan in those days—volatile and earnest, no doubt bringing to his companions the experience of real suffering, a veteran among cadets. His parents had died—his father had been a banker with the foresight to keep a small account in Switzerland. There had not been much, but enough to see him through Oxford, and protect him from the cold wind of poverty.

Smiley remembered so well that interview with Fennan; one among many, yet different. Different because of the language. Fennan was so articulate, so quick, so sure. "Their greatest day," he had said, "was when the miners came. They came from the Rhondda, you know, and to the comrades it seemed the spirit of Freedom had come down with them from the hills. It was a hunger march. It never seemed to occur to the Group that the marchers might actually *be* hungry, but it occurred to me. We hired a truck and the girls made stew—tons of it. We got the meat cheap from a sympathetic butcher in the market. We drove the truck out to meet them. They ate the stew and marched on. They didn't like us really you know, didn't trust us." He laughed. "They were so small—that's what I remember best—small and dark like elves. We hoped they'd sing and they did. But not for us—for themselves. That was the first time I had met Welshmen.

"It made me understand my own race better, I think—I'm a Jew, you know."

Smiley had nodded.

"They didn't know what to do when the Welshmen had gone. What do you do when a dream has come

63

true? They realised then why the Party didn't much care about intellectuals. I think they felt cheap, mostly, and ashamed. Ashamed of their beds and their rooms, their full bellies and their clever essays. Ashamed of their talents and their humour. They were always saying how Keir Hardie taught himself shorthand with a piece of chalk on the coal face, you know. They were ashamed of having pencils and paper. But it's no good just throwing them away, is it? That's what I learnt in the end. That's why I left the Party, I suppose."

Smiley wanted to ask him how Fennan himself had felt, but Fennan was talking again. He had shared nothing with them, he had come to realise that. They were not men, but children, who dreamed of freedom-fires, gipsy music and one world tomorrow, who rode on white horses across the Bay of Biscay or with a child's pleasure bought beer for starving elves from Wales; children who had no power to resist the Eastern sun, and obediently turned their tousled heads towards it. They loved each other and believed they loved mankind, they fought each other and believed they fought the world.

Soon he found them comic and touching. To him, they might as well have knitted socks for soldiers. The disproportion between the dream and reality drove him to a close examination of both; he put all his energy into philosophical and historical reading, and found, to his surprise, comfort and peace in the intellectual purity of Marxism. He feasted on its intellectual ruthlessness, was thrilled by its fearlessness, its academic reversal of traditional values. In the end it was this and not the Party that gave him strength in his solitude, a philosophy which exacted total sacrifice to an unassailable formula, which humiliated and inspired him; and when he finally found success, prosperity and integration, he turned his back sadly upon it as a treasure he had outgrown and must leave at Oxford with the days of his youth.

This was how Fennan had described it and Smiley

had understood. It was scarcely the story of anger and resentment that Smiley had come to expect in such interviews, but (perhaps because of that) it seemed more real. There was another thing about that interview: Smiley's conviction that Fennan had left something important unsaid.

Was there any *factual* connection between the incident in Bywater Street and Fennan's death? Smiley reproached himself for being carried away. Seen in perspective, there was nothing but the sequence of events to suggest that Fennan and Smiley were part of a single problem.

The sequence of events, that is, and the weight of Smiley's intuition, experience or what you will—the extra sense that had told him to ring the bell and not use his key, the sense that did not, however, warn him that a murderer stood in the night with a piece of lead piping.

The interview had been informal, that was true. The walk in the park reminded him more of Oxford than of Whitehall. The walk in the park, the café in Millbank—yes, there had been a procedural difference too, but what did it amount to? An official of the Foreign Office walking in the park, talking earnestly with an anonymous little man . . . Unless the little man was *not* anonymous!

Smiley took a paper-back book and began to write in pencil on the fly-leaf:

"Let us assume what is by no means proven: that the murder of Fennan and the attempted murder of Smiley *are* related. What circumstances connected Smiley with Fennan *before* Fennan's death?

1. Before the interview on Monday, 2nd January, I had never met Fennan. I read his file at the Department and I had certain preliminary enquiries made.
2. On 2nd January I went alone to the Foreign Office by taxi. The F.O. arranged the interview,

but did not, repeat not, know in advance who
would conduct it. Fennan therefore had no prior
knowledge of my identity, nor had anyone else
outside the Department.

3. The interview fell into two parts; the first at the
F.O., when people wandered through the room
and took no notice of us at all, the second outside
when anyone could have seen us."

What followed? Nothing, unless . . .

Yes, that was the only possible conclusion: unless
whoever saw them together recognised not only Fennan
but Smiley as well, and was violently opposed to their
association.

Why? In what way was Smiley dangerous? His eyes
suddenly opened very wide. Of course—in one way, in
one way only—*as a security officer.*

He put down his pencil.

And so whoever killed Sam Fennan was anxious that
he should not talk to a security officer. Someone in the
Foreign Office, perhaps. But essentially someone who
knew Smiley too. Someone Fennan had known at Oxford, known as a communist, someone who feared ex-
posure, who thought that Fennan would talk, had talked
already, perhaps? And if he had talked already then of
course Smiley would have to be killed—killed quickly
before he could put in his report.

That would explain the murder of Fennan and the
assault on Smiley. It made some sense, but not much.
He had built a card-house as high as it would go, and
he still had cards in his hand. What about Elsa, her
lies, her complicity, her fear? What about the car and
the 8.30 call? What about the anonymous letter? If the
murderer was frightened of contact between Smiley and
Fennan, he would scarcely call attention to Fennan by
denouncing him. Who then? Who?

He lay back and closed his eyes. His head was throbbing again. Perhaps Peter Guillam could help. He was
the only hope. His head was going round. It hurt terribly.

IX

TIDYING UP

Mendel showed Peter Guillam into the ward, grinning hugely.

"Got him," he said.

The conversation was awkward; strained for Guillam at least, by the recollection of Smiley's abrupt resignation and the incongruity of meeting in a hospital ward. Smiley was wearing a blue bedjacket, his hair was spiky and untidy above the bandages and he still had the trace of a heavy bruise on his left temple.

After a particularly awkward pause, Smiley said: "Look, Peter, Mendel's told you what happened to me. You're the expert—what do we know about the East German Steel Mission?"

"Pure as the driven snow, dear boy, except for their sudden departure. Only about three men and a dog in the thing. They hung out in Hampstead somewhere. No one quite knew why they were here when they first came but they've done quite a decent job in the last four years."

"What are their terms of reference?"

"God knows. I think they thought when they arrived that they were going to persuade the Board of Trade to break the European steel rings, but they got the cold shoulder. Then they went in for consular stuff with the accent on machine tools and finished products, exchange of industrial and technical information and so on. Nothing to do with what they came for but rather more acceptable, I gather."

"Who were they?"

"Oh—couple of technicians—Professor Doktor someone and Doktor someone else—couple of girls and a general dogsbody."

"Who was the dogsbody?"

"Don't know. Some young diplomat to iron out the wrinkles. We have them recorded at the Department. I can send you details, I suppose."

"If you don't mind."

"No, of course not."

There was another awkward pause. Smiley said: "Photographs would be a help, Peter. Could you manage that?"

"Yes, yes, of course." Guillam looked away from Smiley in some embarrassment. "We don't know much about the East Germans really, you know. We get odd bits here and there, but on the whole they're something of a mystery. If they operate at all they don't do it under Trade or Diplomatic cover—that's why, if you're right about this chap, it's so odd him coming from the Steel Mission."

"Oh," said Smiley, flatly.

"How do they operate?" asked Mendel.

"It's hard to generalise from the very few isolated cases we do know of. My impression is that they run their agents direct from Germany with no contact between controller and agent in the operational zone."

"But that must limit them terribly," cried Smiley. "You may have to wait months before your agent can travel to a meeting place outside his own country. He may not have the necessary cover to make the journey at all."

"Well, obviously it does limit him, but their targets seem to be so insignificant. They prefer to run foreign nationals—Swedes, expatriate Poles and what not, on

68

short-term missions, where the limitations of their technique don't matter. In exceptional cases where they have an agent resident in the target country, they work on a courier system, which corresponds to the Soviet pattern."

Smiley was listening now.

"As a matter of fact," Guillam went on, "the Americans intercepted a courier quite recently, which is where we learnt the little we do know about G.D.R. technique."

"Such as what?"

"Oh well, never waiting at a rendezvous, never meeting at the stated time but twenty minutes before; recognition signals—all the usual conjuring tricks that give a gloss to low grade information. They muck about with names, too. A courier may have to contact three or four agents—a controller may run as many as fifteen. They never invent cover names for themselves."

"What do you mean? Surely they must."

"They get the agent to do it for them. The agent chooses a name, any name he likes, and the controller adopts it. A gimmick really—" he stopped, looking at Mendel in surprise.

Mendel had leapt to his feet.

Guillam sat back in his chair and wondered if he were allowed to smoke. He decided reluctantly that he wasn't. He could have done with a cigarette.

"Well?" said Smiley. Mendel had described to Guillam his interview with Mr. Scarr.

"It fits," said Guillam. "Obviously it fits with what we know. But then we don't know all that much. If Blondie was a courier, it is exceptional—in my experience at least—that he should use a trade delegation as a staging post."

"You said the Mission had been here four years," said Mendel. "Blondie first came to Scarr four years ago."

No one spoke for a moment. Then Smiley said earnestly: "Peter, it is possible, isn't it? I mean they might under certain operational conditions need to have a station over here as well as couriers."

"Well, of course, if they were on to something really big they might."

"Meaning if they had a highly placed resident agent in play?"

"Yes, roughly."

"And assuming they had such an agent, a Maclean or Fuchs, it is conceivable that they would establish a station here under trade cover with no operational function except to hold the agent's hand?"

"Yes, it's conceivable. But it's a tall order, George. What you're suggesting is that the agent is run from abroad, serviced by courier and the courier is serviced by the Mission, which is also the agent's personal guardian angel. He'd have to be some agent."

"I'm not suggesting quite that—but near enough. And I accept that the system demands a high-grade agent. Don't forget we only have Blondie's word for it that he came from abroad."

Mendel chipped in: "This agent—would he be in touch with the Mission direct?"

"Good lord, no," said Guillam. "He'd probably have an emergency procedure for getting in touch with them—a telephone code or something of the sort."

"How does that work?" asked Mendel.

"Varies. Might be on the wrong number system. You dial the number from a call box and ask to speak to George Brown. You're told George Brown doesn't live there so you apologise and ring off. The time and the rendezvous are prearranged—the emergency signal is contained in the name you ask for. Someone will be there."

"What else would the Mission do?" asked Smiley.

"Hard to say. Pay him probably. Arrange a collecting place for reports. The controller would make all those arrangements for the agent, of course, and tell him his part of it by courier. They work on the Soviet principle a good deal, as I told you—even the smallest details are arranged by control. The people in the field are allowed very little independence."

There was another silence. Smiley looked at Guillam and then at Mendel, then blinked and said:

"Blondie didn't come to Scarr in January and February, did he?"

"No," said Mendel; "this was the first year."

"Fennan always went skiing in January and February. This was the first time in four years he'd missed."

"I wonder," said Smiley; "whether I ought to go and see Maston again."

Guillam stretched luxuriously and smiled: "You can always try. He'll be thrilled to hear you've been brained. I've a sneaking feeling he'll think Battersea's on the coast, but not to worry. Tell him you were attacked while wandering about in someone's private yard—he'll understand. Tell him about your assailant, too, George. You've never seen him, mind, and you don't know his name, but he's a courier of the East German Intelligence Service. Maston will back you up; he always does. Specially when he's got to report to the Minister."

Smiley looked at Guillam and said nothing.

"After your bang on the head, too," Guillam added; "he'll understand."

"But, Peter—"

"I know, George, I know."

"Well, let me tell you another thing. Blondie collected his car on the first Tuesday of each month."

"So?"

"Those were the nights Elsa Fennan went to the Weybridge Rep. Fennan worked late on Tuesdays, she said."

Guillam got up. "Let me dig about, George. Cheerio Mendel, I'll probably give you a ring tonight. I don't see what we can do now, anyway, but it would be nice to know, wouldn't it?" He reached the door. "Incidentally,

71

where are Fennan's possessions—wallet, diary and so forth? Stuff they found on the body?"

"Probably still at the Station," said Mendel; "until after the inquest."

Guillam stood looking at Smiley for a moment, wondering what to say.

"Anything you want, George?"

"No thanks—Oh, there is one thing."

"Yes?"

"Could you get the C.I.D. off my back? They've visited me three times now and of course they've got nowhere locally. Could you make this an Intelligence matter for the time being? Be mysterious and soothing?"

"Yes, I should think so."

"I know it's difficult, Peter, because I'm not—"

"Oh another thing just to cheer you up. I had that comparison made between Fennan's suicide note and the anonymous letter. They were done by different people on the same machine. Different pressures and spacing but identical type face. So long, old dear. Tuck into the grapes."

Guillam closed the door behind him. They heard his footsteps echoing crisply down the bare corridor.

Mendel rolled himself a cigarette.

"Lord," said Smiley; "does nothing frighten you? Haven't you seen the Sister here?"

Mendel grinned and shook his head.

"You can only die once," he said, putting the cigarette between his thin lips. Smiley watched him light it. He produced his lighter, took the hood off it and rotated the wheel with his stained thumb, swiftly cupping both hands around it and nursing the flame towards the cigarette. There might have been a hurricane blowing.

"Well, you're the crime expert," said Smiley. "How are we doing?"

"Messy," said Mendel. "Untidy."

"Why?"

"Loose ends everywhere. No police work. Nothing checked. Like algebra."

"What's algebra got to do with it?"

"You've got to prove what *can* be proved, first. Find the constants. Did she really go to the theatre? Was she alone? Did the neighbours hear her come back? If so, what time? Was Fennan really late Tuesdays? Did his Missus go to the theatre regular *every* fortnight like she said?"

"And the 8.30 call. Can you tidy that for me?"

"You've got that call on the brain, haven't you?"

"Yes. Of all the loose ends, that's the loosest. I brood over it, you know, and there just isn't any sense in it. I've been through his train timetable. He was a punctual man—often got to the F.O. before anyone else, unlocked his own cupboard. He would have caught the 8.45, the 9.08 or at worst the 9.14. The 8.45 got him in at 9.38—he liked to be at his office by a quarter to ten. He couldn't possibly want to be woken at 8.30."

"Perhaps he just liked bells," said Mendel, getting up.

"And the letters," Smiley continued. "Different typists but the same machine. Discounting the murderer two people had access to that machine: Fennan and his wife. If we accept that Fennan typed the suicide note—and he certainly signed it—we must accept that it was Elsa who typed the denunciation. Why did she do that?"

Smiley was tired out, relieved that Mendel was going.

"Off to tidy up. Find the constants."

"You'll need money," said Smiley, and offered him some from the wallet beside his bed. Mendel took it without ceremony, and left.

Smiley lay back. His head was throbbing madly, burning hot. He thought of calling the nurse and cowardice prevented him. Gradually the throbbing eased. He heard from outside the ringing of an ambulance bell as it turned off Prince of Wales Drive into the hospital yard. "Perhaps he just liked bells," he muttered, and fell asleep.

He was woken by the sound of argument in the corridor—he heard the Sister's voice raised in protest; he heard footsteps and Mendel's voice, urgent in contradiction. The door opened suddenly and someone put the light on. He blinked and sat up, glancing at his watch. It was a quarter to six. Mendel was talking to him, almost shouting. What was he trying to say? Something about Battersea Bridge . . . the river police . . . missing since yesterday. . . . He was wide awake. Adam Scarr was dead.

X

THE VIRGIN'S STORY

Mendel drove very well, with a kind of school ma'amish pedantry that Smiley would have found comic. The Weybridge road was packed with traffic as usual. Mendel hated motorists. Give a man a car of his own and he leaves humility and common sense behind him in the garage. He didn't care who it was—he'd seen bishops in purple doing seventy in a built-up area, frightening pedestrians out of their wits. He liked Smiley's car. He liked the fussy way it had been maintained, the sensible extras, wing mirrors and reversing light. It was a decent little car.

He liked people who looked after things, who finished what they began. He liked thoroughness and precision. No skimping. Like this murderer. What had Scarr said? "Young, mind, but cool. Cool as charity." He knew that look, and Scarr had known it too . . . the look of complete negation that reposes in the eyes of a young killer. Not the look of a wild beast, not the grinning savagery of a maniac, but the look born of supreme efficiency, tried and proven. It was a stage beyond the experience of war. The witnessing of death in war brings a sophistication of its own; but beyond that, far beyond, is the conviction of supremacy in the heart of the professional killer. Yes, Mendel had seen it before: the one that stood apart from the gang, pale eyed, expressionless, the one the girls went after, spoke of without smiling. Yes, he was a cool one all right.

Scarr's death had frightened Mendel. He made Smiley promise not to go back to Bywater Street when he was released from hospital. With any luck they'd think he was dead, anyway. Scarr's death proved one thing, of course: the murderer was still in England, still anxious to tidy up. "When I get up," Smiley had said last night, "we must get him out of his hole again. Put out bits of cheese." Mendel knew who the cheese would be: Smiley. Of course if they were right about the motive there would be other cheese too: Fennan's wife. In fact, Mendel thought grimly, it doesn't say much for her that she hasn't been murdered. He felt ashamed of himself and turned his mind to other things. Such as Smiley again.

Odd little beggar, Smiley was. Reminded Mendel of a fat boy he'd played football with at school. Couldn't run, couldn't kick, blind as a bat but played like hell, never satisfied till he'd got himself torn to bits. Used to box, too. Came in wide open, swinging his arms about: got himself half killed before the referee stopped it. Clever bloke, too.

Mendel stopped at a roadside café for a cup of tea and a bun, then drove into Weybridge. The Repertory Theatre was in a one way street leading off the High Street where parking was impossible. Finally he left the car at the railway station and walked back into the town.

The front doors of the theatre were locked. Mendel walked round to the side of the building under a brick archway. A green door was propped open. It had push bars on the inside and the words "stage door" scribbled in chalk. There was no bell; a faint smell of coffee issued from the dark green corridor within. Mendel stepped through the doorway and walked down the corridor, at the end of which he found a stone staircase with a metal handrail leading upwards to another green door. The smell of coffee was stronger, and he heard the sound of voices.

"Oh rot, darling, frankly. If the culture vultures of blissful Surrey want Barrie three months running let them have it, say I. It's either Barrie or 'A Cuckoo in the Nest' for the third year running and for me Barrie gets it by a short head"—this from a middle-aged female voice.

A querulous male replied: "Well, Ludo can always do Peter Pan, can't you Ludo?"

"Bitchie, bitchie," said a third voice, also male, and Mendel opened the door.

He was standing in the wings of the stage. On his left was a piece of thick hardboard with about a dozen switches mounted on a wooden panel. An absurd rococo chair in gilt and embroidery stood beneath it for the prompter and factotum.

In the middle of the stage two men and a woman sat on barrels smoking and drinking coffee. The décor represented the deck of a ship. A mast with rigging and rope ladders occupied the centre of the stage, and a large cardboard cannon pointed disconsolately towards a backcloth of sea and sky.

The conversation stopped abruptly as Mendel appeared on the stage. Someone murmured: "My dear, the ghost at the feast," and they all looked at him and giggled.

The woman spoke first: "Are you looking for someone, dear?"

"Sorry to butt in. Wanted to talk about becoming a subscriber to the theatre. Join the club."

"Why yes, of course. How nice," she said, getting up and walking over to him; "How *very* nice." She took his left hand in both her own and squeezed it, stepping back at the same time and extending her arms to their full length. It was her chatelaine gesture—Lady Macbeth receives Duncan. She put her head on one side and smiled girlishly, retained his hand and led him across the stage to the opposite wing. A door led into a tiny office littered with old programmes and posters, grease-paint, false hair and tawdry pieces of nautical costume.

"Have you seen our panto this year? 'Treasure Island.' Such a *gratifying* success. And so much more *social content,* don't you think, than those vulgar nursery tales?"

Mendel said: "Yes, wasn't it," without the least idea of what she was talking about, when his eye caught a pile of bills rather neatly assembled and held together by a bull-dog clip. The top one was made out to Mrs. Ludo Oriel and was four months overdue.

She was looking at him shrewdly through her glasses. She was small and dark, with lines on her neck and a great deal of make-up. The lines under her eyes had been levelled off with greasepaint but the effect had not lasted. She was wearing slacks and a chunky pullover liberally splashed with distemper. She smoked incessantly. Her mouth was very long, and as she held her cigarette in the middle of it in a direct line beneath her nose, her lips formed an exaggerated convex curve, distorting the lower half of her face and giving her an ill-tempered and impatient look. Mendel thought she would probably be difficult and clever. It was a relief to think she couldn't pay her bills.

"You *do* want to join the club, don't you?"

"No."

She suddenly flew into a rage: "If you're another bloody tradesman you can get out. I've said I'll pay and I will, just don't pester me. If you let people think I'm finished I *will* be and you'll be the losers, not me."

"I'm not a creditor, Mrs. Oriel. I've come to offer you money."

She was waiting.

"I'm a divorce agent. Rich client. Like to ask you a few questions. We're prepared to pay for your time."

"Christ," she said with relief. "Why didn't you say so in the first place?" They both laughed. Mendel put five pounds on top of the bills, counting them down.

"Now," said Mendel; "how do you keep your club subscription list? What are the benefits of joining?"

"Well, we have watery coffee on stage every morning at eleven sharp. Members of the club can mix with the cast during the break between rehearsals from 11.00 to 11.45. They pay for whatever they have, of course, but entry is strictly limited to club members."

"Quite."

"That's probably the part that interests you. We seem to get nothing but pansies and nymphos in the morning."

"It may be. What else goes on?"

"We put on a different show each fortnight. Members can reserve seats for a particular day of each run—the second Wednesday of each run, and so on. We always begin a run on the first and third Mondays of the month. The show begins at 7.30 and we hold the club reservations until 7.20. The girl at the box office has the seating plan and strikes off each seat as it's sold. Club reservations are marked in red and aren't sold off till last."

"I see. So if one of your members doesn't take his usual seat, it would be marked off on the seating plan."

"Only if it's sold."

"Of course."

"We're not often full after the first week. We're trying to do a show a week, you see, but it's not easy to get the—er—facilities. There isn't the support for two-week runs really."

"No, no, quite. Do you keep old seating plans?"

"Sometimes, for the accounts."

"How about Tuesday the third of January?"

She opened a cupboard and took out a sheaf of printed seating plans. "This is the second fortnight of our pantomime, of course. Tradition."

"Quite," said Mendel.

"Now who is it you're so interested in?" asked Mrs. Oriel, picking up a ledger from the desk.

"Small blonde party, aged about forty-two or three. Name of Fennan, Elsa Fennan."

Mrs. Oriel opened her ledger. Mendel quite shamelessly looked over her shoulder. The names of club members were entered neatly in the left-hand column. A red tick on the extreme left of the page indicated that the member had paid his subscription. On the right-hand side of the page were notes of standing reservations made for the year. There were about eighty members.

"Name doesn't ring a bell. Where does she sit?"

"No idea."

"Oh, yes, here we are. Merridale Lane, Walliston. Merridale!—I *ask* you. Let's look. A rear stall at the end of a row. Very odd choice, don't you think? Seat number R2. But God knows whether she took it on 3rd January. I shouldn't think we've got the plan any more, though I've never thrown anything away in my life. Things just evaporate, don't they?" She looked at him out of the corner of her eye, wondering whether she'd earned her five pounds. "Tell you what, we'll ask the Virgin." She got up and walked to the door; "Fennan . . . Fennan. . . ." she said. "Half a sec, that does ring a bell. I wonder why. Well I'm damned—of course—the music case." She opened the door. "Where's the Virgin?" she said, talking to someone on the stage.

"God knows."

"Helpful pig," said Mrs. Oriel, and closed the door again. She turned to Mendel: "The Virgin's our white hope. English rose, local solicitor's stage-struck daughter, all lisle stockings and get-me-if-you-can. We loathe her. She gets a part occasionally because her father pays tuition fees. She does seating in the evenings sometimes when there's a rush—she and Mrs. Torr, the cleaner, who does cloaks. When things are quiet, Mrs. Torr does the whole thing and the Virgin mopes about in the wings hoping the female lead will drop dead." She paused. "I'm damned sure I remember 'Fennan.' Damn sure I do. I wonder where that cow *is*." She disappeared for a couple of minutes and returned with a tall and rather pretty girl with fuzzy blonde hair and pink cheeks—good at tennis and swimming.

"This is Elizabeth Pidgeon. She may be able to help.

Darling, we want to find out a Mrs. Fennan, a club member. Didn't you tell me something about her?"

"Oh, *yes*, Ludo." She must have thought she sounded sweet. She smiled vapidly at Mendel, put her head on one side and twined her fingers together. Mendel jerked his head towards her.

"Do you know her?" asked Mrs. Oriel.

"Oh *yes*, Ludo. She's madly musical; at least I think she must be because she always brings her music. She's madly thin and odd. She's foreign, isn't she, Ludo?"

"Why odd?" asked Mendel.

"Oh, well, last time she came she got in a frightful pet about the seat next to her. It was a club reservation you see and simply hours after twenty past. We'd just started the panto season and there were millions of people wanting seats so I let it go. She kept on saying she was sure the person would come because he always did."

"Did he?" asked Mendel.

"No. I let the seat go. She must have been in an awful pet because she left after the second act, and forgot to collect her music case."

"This person she was so sure would turn up," said Mendel; "is he friendly with Mrs. Fennan?"

Ludo Oriel gave Mendel a suggestive wink.

"Well, gosh, I should think *so*, he's her husband, isn't he?"

Mendel looked at her for a minute and then smiled: "Couldn't we find a chair for Elizabeth?" he said.

"Gosh, thanks," said the Virgin, and sat on the edge of an old gilt chair like the prompter's chair in the wings. She put her red, fat hands on her knees and leaned forward, smiling all the time, thrilled to be the centre of so much interest. Mrs. Oriel looked at her venomously.

"What makes you think he was her husband, Elizabeth?" There was an edge to his voice which had not been there before.

"Well, I know they arrive separately, but I thought that as they had seats apart from the rest of the club

81

reservations, they must be husband and wife. And of course he always brings a music case too."

"I see. What else can you remember about that evening, Elizabeth?"

"Oh, well, lots really because you see I felt awful about her leaving in such a pet and then later that night she rang up. Mrs. Fennan did, I mean. She said her name and said she'd left early and forgotten her music case. She'd lost the ticket for it, too, and was in a frightful state. It sounded as if she was crying. I heard someone's voice in the background, and then she said someone would drop in and get it if that would be all right without the ticket. I said of course, and half an hour later the man came. He's rather super. Tall and fair."

"I see," said Mendel; "thank you very much, Elizabeth, you've been very helpful."

"Gosh, that's O.K." She got up.

"Incidentally," said Mendel. "This man who collected her music case—he wasn't by any chance the same man who sits beside her in the theatre, was he?"

"Rather. Gosh, sorry, I should have said that."

"Did you talk to him?"

"Well, just to say here you are, sort of thing."

"What kind of voice had he?"

"Oh, foreign, like Mrs. Fennan's—she *is* foreign, isn't she? That's what I put it down to—all her fuss and state—foreign temperament."

She smiled at Mendel, waited a moment then walked out like Alice.

"Cow," said Mrs. Oriel, looking at the closed door. Her eyes turned to Mendel. "Well, I hope you've got your five quids' worth."

"I think so," said Mendel.

XI

THE UNRESPECTABLE CLUB

Mendel found Smiley sitting in an armchair fully dressed. Peter Guillam was stretched luxuriously on the bed, a pale green folder held casually in his hand. Outside, the sky was black and menacing.

"Enter the third murderer," said Guillam as Mendel walked in. Mendel sat down at the end of the bed and nodded happily to Smiley, who looked pale and depressed.

"Congratulations. Nice to see you on your feet."

"Thank you. I'm afraid if you did see me on my feet you wouldn't congratulate me. I feel as weak as a kitten."

"When are they letting you go?"

"I don't know when they expect me to go—"

"Haven't you asked?"

"No."

"Well, you'd better. I've got news for you. I don't know what it means but it means something."

"Well, well," said Guillam; "everyone's got news for everyone else. Isn't that exciting. George has been looking at my family snaps"—he raised the green folder a fraction of an inch—"and recognises all his old chums."

Mendel felt baffled and rather left out of things. Smiley intervened: "I'll tell you all about it over dinner to-morrow evening. I'm getting out of here in the morning, whatever they say. I think we've found the murderer and a lot more besides. Now let's have your news." There was no triumph in his eyes. Only anxiety.

Membership of the club to which Smiley belonged is not quoted among the respectable acquisitions of those who adorn the pages of "Who's Who." It was formed by a young renegade of the Junior Carlton named Steed-Asprey, who had been warned off by the Secretary for blaspheming within the hearing of a South African bishop. He persuaded his former Oxford landlady to leave her quiet house in Hollywell and take over two rooms and a cellar in Manchester Square which a mon-ied relative put at his disposal. It had once had forty members who each paid fifty guineas a year. There were thirty-one left. There were no women and no rules, no secretary and no bishops. You could take sandwiches and buy a bottle of beer, you could take sandwiches and buy nothing at all. As long as you were reasonably sober and minded your own business, no one gave twopence what you wore, did or said, or whom you brought with you. Mrs. Sturgeon no longer devilled at the bar, or brought you your chop in front of the fire in the cellar, but presided in genial comfort over the ministrations of two retired sergeants from a small border regiment.

Naturally enough, most of the members were approx-imate contemporaries of Smiley at Oxford. It had al-ways been agreed that the club was to serve one genera-tion only, that it would grow old and die with its members. The war had taken its toll of Jebedee and others, but no one had ever suggested they should elect new members. Besides, the premises were now their own, Mrs. Sturgeon's future had been taken care of and the club was solvent.

It was a Saturday evening and only half a dozen peo-ple were there. Smiley had ordered their meal, and a table was set for them in the cellar, where a bright coal fire burned in a brick hearth. They were alone, there was sirloin and claret; outside the rain fell continuously. For all three of them the world seemed an untroubled and decent place that night, despite the strange business that brought them together.

"To make sense of what I have to tell you," began Smiley at last, addressing himself principally to Mendel, "I shall have to talk at length about myself. I'm an intelligence officer by trade as you know—I've been in the Service since the Flood, long before we were mixed up in power politics with Whitehall. In those days we were understaffed and underpaid. After the usual training and probation in South America and Central Europe, I took a job lecturing at a German University, talent spotting for young Germans with an agent potential." He paused, smiled at Mendel and said: "Forgive the jargon." Mendel nodded solemnly and Smiley went on. He knew he was being pompous, and didn't know how to prevent himself.

"It was shortly before the last war, a terrible time in Germany then, intolerance run mad. I would have been a lunatic to approach anyone myself. My only chance was to be as nondescript as I could, politically and socially colourless, and to put forward candidates for recruitment by someone else. I tried to bring some back to England for short periods on students' tours. I made a point of having no contact at all with the Department when I came over because we hadn't any idea in those days of the efficiency of German Counter Intelligence. I never knew who was approached, and of course it was much better that way. In case I was blown, I mean.

"My story really begins in 1938. I was alone in my rooms one summer evening. It had been a beautiful day, warm and peaceful. Fascism might never have been heard of. I was working in my shirt sleeves at a desk by my window, not working very hard because it was such a wonderful evening."

He paused, embarrassed for some reason, and fussed

a little with the port. Two pink spots appeared high on his cheeks. He felt slightly drunk though he had had very little wine.

"To resume," he said, and felt an ass: "I'm sorry, I feel a little inarticulate . . . Anyway, as I sat there, there was a knock on the door and a young student came in. He was nineteen, in fact, but he looked younger. His name was Dieter Frey. He was a pupil of mine, an intelligent boy and remarkable to look at." Smiley paused again, staring before him. Perhaps it was his illness, his weakness, which brought the memory so vividly before him.

"Dieter was a very handsome boy, with a high forehead and a lot of unruly black hair. The lower part of his body was deformed, I think by infantile paralysis. He carried a stick and leaned heavily upon it when he walked. Naturally he cut a rather romantic figure at a small university; they thought him Byronic and so on. In fact I could never find him romantic myself. The Germans have a passion for discovering young genius, you know, from Herder to Stefan George—somebody lionised them practically from the cradle. But you couldn't lionise Dieter. There was a fierce independence, a ruthlessness about him which scared off the most determined patron. This defensiveness in Dieter derived not only from his deformity, but his race, which was Jewish. How on earth he kept his place at University I could never understand. It was possible that they didn't know he was a Jew—his beauty might have been southern, I suppose, Italian, but I don't really see how. To me he was obviously Jewish.

"Dieter was a socialist. He made no secret of his views even in those days. I once considered him for recruitment, but it seemed futile to take on anyone who was so obviously earmarked for concentration camp. Besides he was too volatile, too swift to react, too brightly painted, too vain. He led all the societies at the University—debating, political, poetry and so on. In all the athletic guilds he held honorary positions. He had the nerve not to drink in a University where you proved your manhood by being drunk most of your first year.

"That was Dieter, then: a tall, handsome, commanding cripple, the idol of his generation; a Jew. And that was the man who came to see me that hot summer evening.

"I sat him down and offered him a drink, which he refused. I made some coffee, I think, on a gas ring. We spoke in a desultory way about my last lecture on Keats. I had complained about the application of German critical methods to English poetry, and this had led to some discussion—as usual—on the Nazi interpretation of 'decadence' in art. Dieter dragged it all up again and became more and more outspoken in his condemnation of modern Germany and finally of Nazism itself. Naturally, I was guarded—I think I was less of a fool in those days than I am now. In the end he asked me point blank what I thought of the Nazis. I replied rather pointedly that I was disinclined to criticise my hosts, and that anyway I didn't think politics were much fun. I shall never forget his reply. He was furious, struggled to his feet and shouted at me: *'Von Freude ist nicht die Rede!'*—'We're not talking about fun!' " Smiley broke off and looked across the table to Guillam: "I'm sorry Peter, I'm being rather long-winded."

"Nonsense, old dear. You tell the story in your own way." Mendel grunted his approval; he was sitting rather stiffly with both hands on the table before him. There was no light in the room now except the bright glow of the fire, which threw tall shadows on the rough-cast wall behind them. The port decanter was three parts empty; Smiley gave himself a little and passed it on.

"He raved at me. He simply did not understand how I could apply an independent standard of criticism to art and remain so insensitive to politics, how I could bleat about artistic freedom when a third of Europe was in chains. Did it mean nothing to me that contemporary civilisation was being bled to death? What was so sacred about the eighteenth century that I could throw the twentieth away? He had come to me because he enjoyed

87

my seminars and thought me an enlightened man, but he now realised that I was worse than all of them.

"I let him go. What else could I do? On paper he was suspect anyway—a rebellious Jew with a University place still mysteriously free. But I watched him. The term was nearly over and the long vacation soon to begin. In the closing debate of the term three days later he was dreadfully outspoken. He really frightened people, you know, and they grew silent and apprehensive. The end of the term came and Dieter departed without a word of farewell to me. I never expected to see him again.

"It was about six months before I did. I had been visiting friends near Dresden, Dieter's home town, and I arrived half an hour early at the station. Rather than hang around on the platform I decided to go for a stroll. A couple of hundred metres from the station was a tall, rather grim seventeenth-century house. There was a small courtyard in front of it with tall iron railings and a wrought-iron gate. It had apparently been converted into a temporary prison: a group of shaven prisoners, men and women, were being exercised in the yard, walking round the perimeter. Two guards stood in the centre with tommy guns. As I watched I caught sight of a familiar figure, taller than the rest, limping, struggling to keep up with them. It was Dieter. They had taken his stick away.

"When I thought about it afterwards, of course, I realised that the Gestapo would scarcely arrest the most popular member of the University while he was still up. I forgot about my train, went back into the town and looked for his parents in the telephone book. I knew his father had been a doctor so it wasn't difficult. I went to the address and only his mother was there. The father had died already in a concentration camp. She wasn't inclined to talk about Dieter, but it appeared that he had not gone to a Jewish prison but to a general one, and ostensibly for 'a period of correction' only. She expected him back in about three months. I left him a message to say I still had some books of his and would be pleased to return them if he would call on me.

"I'm afraid the events of 1939 must have got the better of me, because I don't believe I gave Dieter another thought that year. Soon after I returned from Dresden my Department ordered me back to England. I packed and left within forty-eight hours, to find London in a turmoil. I was given a new assignment which required intensive preparation, briefing and training. I was to go back to Europe at once and activate almost untried agents in Germany who had been recruited against such an emergency. I began to memorise the dozen odd names and addresses. You can imagine my reaction when I discovered Dieter Frey among them.

"When I read his file I found he had more or less recruited himself by bursting in on the consulate in Dresden and demanding to know why no one lifted a finger to stop the persecution of the Jews." Smiley paused and laughed to himself; "Dieter was a great one for getting people to do things." He glanced quickly at Mendel and Guillam. Both had their eyes fixed on him.

"I suppose my first reaction was pique. The boy had been right under my nose and I hadn't considered him suitable—what was some ass in Dresden up to? And then I was alarmed to have this firebrand on my hands, whose impulsive temperament could cost me and others our lives. Despite the slight changes in my appearance and the new cover under which I was operating, I should obviously have to declare myself to Dieter as plain George Smiley from the University, so he could blow me sky high. It seemed a most unfortunate beginning, and I was half resolved to set up my network without Dieter. In the event I was wrong. He was a magnificent agent.

"He didn't curb his flamboyance, but used it skilfully as a kind of double bluff. His deformity kept him out of the Services and he found himself a clerical job on the railways. In no time he worked his way to a position of real responsibility and the quantity of information he obtained was fantastic. Details of troop and ammunition transports, their destination and date of transit. Later he reported on the effectiveness of our bombing, pin-pointed key targets. He was a brilliant organiser and I think that was what saved him. He did a wonderful job on the railways, made himself indispensable, worked all hours of the night and day; became almost inviolate. They even gave him a civilian decoration for exceptional merit and I suppose the Gestapo conveniently lost his file.

"Dieter had a theory that was pure Faust. Thought alone was valueless. You must act for thought to become effective. He used to say that the greatest mistake man ever made was to distinguish between the mind and the body: an order does not exist if it is not obeyed. He used to quote Kleist a great deal: 'if all eyes were made of green glass, and if all that seems white was really green, who would be the wiser?' Something like that.

"As I say, Dieter was a magnificent agent. He even went so far as to arrange for certain freights to be transported on good flying nights for the convenience of our bombers. He had tricks all his own—a natural genius for the nuts and bolts of espionage. It seemed absurd to suppose it could last, but the effect of our bombing was often so widespread that it would have been childish to attribute it to one person's betrayal—let alone to a man so notoriously outspoken as Dieter.

"Where he was concerned my job was easy. Dieter put in a lot of travelling as it was—he had a special pass to get him around. Communication was child's play by comparison with some agents. Occasionally we would actually meet and talk in a café, or he would pick me up in a Ministry car and drive me sixty or seventy miles along a main road, as if he were giving me a lift. But more often we would take a journey in the same train and swap briefcases in the corridor or go to the theatre with parcels and exchange cloakroom tickets. He seldom gave me actual reports but just carbon copies of transit orders. He got his secretary to do a lot—he made her keep a special float which he 'destroyed' every three months by emptying it into his briefcase in the lunch hour.

"Well, in 1943 I was recalled. My trade cover was rather thin by then I think, and I was getting a bit shopsoiled." He stopped and took a cigarette from Guillam's case.

"But don't let's get Dieter out of perspective," he said: "He was my best agent, but he wasn't my only one. I had a lot of headaches of my own—running him was a picnic by comparison with some. When the war was over I tried to find out from my successor what had become of Dieter and the rest of them. Some were resettled in Australia and Canada, some just drifted away to what was left of their home towns. Dieter hesitated, I gather. The Russians were in Dresden, of course, and he may have had doubts. In the end he went—he had to really, because of his mother. He hated the Americans, anyway. And of course he was a socialist.

"I heard later that he had made his career there. The administrative experience he had picked up during the war got him some Government job in the new republic. I suppose that his reputation as a rebel and the suffering of his family cleared the way for him. He must have done pretty well for himself."

"Why?" asked Mendel.

"He was over here until a month ago running the Steel Mission."

"That's not all," said Guillam quickly. "In case you think your cup is full, Mendel, I spared you another visit to Weybridge this morning and called on Elizabeth Pidgeon. It was George's idea." He turned to Smiley: "She's a sort of Moby Dick isn't she—bit white man-eating whale."

"Well?" said Mendel.

"I showed her a picture of that young diplomat by the name of Mundt they kept in tow there to pick up the bits. Elizabeth recognised him at once as the nice man who collected Elsa Fennan's music case. Isn't that jolly?"

"But—"

"I know what you're going to ask, you clever youth. You want to know whether George recognised him too. Well, George did. It's the same nasty fellow who tried to lure him into his own house in Bywater Street. Doesn't he get around?"

Mendel drove to Mitcham. Smiley was dead tired. It was raining again and cold. Smiley hugged his greatcoat round him and, despite his tiredness, watched with quiet pleasure the busy London night go by. He had always loved travelling. Even now, if he had the choice, he would cross France by train rather than fly. He could still respond to the magic noises of a night journey across Europe, the oddly cacophonous chimes and the French voices suddenly waking him from English dreams. Ann had loved it too and they had twice travelled overland to share the dubious joys of that uncomfortable journey.

When they got back Smiley went straight to bed while Mendel made some tea. They drank it in Smiley's bedroom.

"What do we do now?" asked Mendel.

"I thought I might go to Walliston tomorrow."

"You ought to spend the day in bed. What do you want to do there?"

"See Elsa Fennan."

"You're not safe on your own. You'd better let me come. I'll sit in the car while you do the talking. She's a Yid, isn't she?"

Smiley nodded.

"My dad was Yid. He never made such a bloody fuss about it."

XII

DREAM FOR SALE

She opened the door and stood looking at him for a moment in silence.

"You could have let me know you were coming," she said.

"I thought it safer not to."

She was silent again. Finally she said: "I don't know what you mean." It seemed to cost her a good deal.

"May I come in?" said Smiley. "We haven't much time."

She looked old and tired, less resilient perhaps. She led him into the drawing-room and with something like resignation indicated a chair.

Smiley offered her a cigarette and took one himself. She was standing by the window. As he looked at her, watched her quick breathing, her feverish eyes, he realised that she had almost lost the power of self-defence.

When he spoke, his voice was gentle, concessive. To Elsa Fennan it must have seemed like a voice she had longed for, irresistible, offering all strength, comfort, compassion and safety. She gradually moved away from the window and her right hand, which had been pressed against the sill, trailed wistfully along it, then fell to her side in a gesture of submission. She sat opposite him, her eyes upon him in complete dependence, like the eyes of a lover.

"You must have been terribly lonely," he said; "No one can stand it for ever. It takes courage, too, and it's so hard to be brave alone. They never understand that, do they? They never know what it costs—the sordid tricks of lying and deceiving, the isolation from ordinary people. They think you can run on their kind of fuel— the flag waving and the music. But you need a different kind of fuel, don't you, when you're alone? You've got to hate, and it needs strength to hate all the time. And what you must love is so remote, so vague when you're not part of it." He paused. Soon, he thought, soon you'll break. He prayed desperately that she would accept him, accept his comfort. He looked at her. Soon she would break.

"I said we hadn't much time. Do you know what I mean?"

She had folded her hands on her lap and was looking down at them. He saw the dark roots of her yellow hair and wondered why on earth she dyed it. She showed no sign of having heard his question.

"When I left you that morning a month ago I drove to my home in London. A man tried to kill me. That night he nearly succeeded—he hit me on the head three or four times. I've just come out of hospital. As it happens I was lucky. Then there was the garage man he hired the car from. The river police recovered his body from the Thames not long ago. There were no signs of violence—he was just full of whisky. They can't understand it—he hadn't been near the river for years. But then we're dealing with a competent man, aren't we? A trained killer. It seems he's trying to remove anyone who can connect him with Samuel Fennan. Or his wife, of course. Then there's that young blonde girl at the Repertory Theatre . . ."

"What are you saying?" she whispered; "What are you trying to tell me?"

Smiley suddenly wanted to hurt her, to break the last

of her will, to remove her utterly as an enemy. For so long she had haunted him as he had lain helpless, had been a mystery and a power.

"What games did you think you were playing, you two? Do you think you can flirt with power like theirs, give a little and not give all? Do you think that *you* can stop the dance—control the strength you give them? What dreams did you cherish, Mrs. Fennan, that had so little of the world in them?"

She buried her face in her hands and he watched the tears run between her fingers. Her body shook with great sobs and her words came slowly, wrung from her.

"No, no dreams. I had no dream but him. He had one dream, yes . . . one great dream." She went on crying, helpless, and Smiley, half in triumph, half in shame, waited for her to speak again. Suddenly she raised her head and looked at him, the tears still running down her cheeks. "Look at me," she said; "What dream did they leave me? I dreamed of long golden hair and they shaved my head, I dreamed of a beautiful body and they broke it with hunger. I have seen what human beings are, how could I believe in a formula for human beings? I said to him, oh I said to him a thousand times; 'only make no laws, no fine theories, no judgments, and the people may love, but give them one theory, let them invent one slogan, and the game begins again.' I told him that. We talked whole nights away. But no, that little boy must have his dream, and if a new world was to be built, Samuel Fennan must build it. I said to him, 'Listen,' I said; 'They have given you all you have, a home, money and trust. Why do you do it to them?' And he said to me: 'I do it *for* them. I am the surgeon and one day they will understand.' He was a child, Mr. Smiley, they led him like a child."

He dared not speak, dared put nothing to the test.

"Five years ago he met that Dieter. In a ski hut near Garmisch. Freitag told us later that Dieter had planned it that way—Dieter couldn't ski anyway because of his legs. Nothing seemed real then; Freitag wasn't a real name. Fennan christened him Freitag like Man Friday in Robinson Crusoe. Dieter found that so funny and afterwards we never talked of Dieter but always of Mr. Robinson and Freitag." She broke off now and looked at him with a very faint smile: "I'm sorry," she said; "I'm not very coherent."

"I understand," said Smiley.

"That girl—what did you say about that girl?"

"She's alive. Don't worry. Go on."

"Fennan liked you, you know. Freitag tried to kill you . . . why?"

"Because I came back, I suppose, and asked you about the 8.30 call. You told Freitag that, didn't you?"

"Oh, God," she said, her fingers at her mouth.

"You rang him up, didn't you? As soon as I'd gone?"

"Yes, yes. I was frightened. I wanted to warn him to go, him and Dieter, to go away and never come back, because I knew you'd find out. If not today than one day, but I knew you'd find out in the end. Why would they never leave me alone? They were frightened of me because they knew I had no dreams, that I only wanted Samuel, wanted him safe to love and care for. They relied on that."

Smiley felt his head throbbing erratically. "So you rang him straight away," he said. "You tried the Primrose number first and couldn't get through."

"Yes," she said vaguely. "Yes, that's right. But they're both Primrose numbers."

"So you rang the *other* number, the alternative . . ."

She drifted back to the window, suddenly exhausted and limp; she seemed happier now—the storm had left her reflective and, in a way, content.

"Yes. Freitag was a great one for alternative plans."

"What was the other number?" Smiley insisted. He watched her anxiously as she stared out of the window into the dark garden.

"Why do you want to know?"

He came and stood beside her at the window, watching her profile. His voice was suddenly harsh and energetic.

"I said the girl was all right. You and I are alive, too. But don't think that's going to last."

She turned to him with fear in her eyes, looked at him for a moment, then nodded. Smiley took her by the arm and guided her to a chair. He ought to make her a hot drink or something. She sat down quite mechanically, almost with the detachment of incipient madness.

"The other number was 9747."

"Any address—did you have an address?"

"No, no address. Only the telephone. Tricks on the telephone. No address," she repeated, with unnatural emphasis, so that Smiley looked at her and wondered. A thought suddenly struck him—a memory of Dieter's skill in communication.

"Freitag didn't meet you the night Fennan died, did he? He didn't come to the theatre?"

"No."

"That was the first time he had missed, wasn't it? You panicked and left early."

"No . . . yes, yes, I panicked."

"No you didn't! You left early because you had to, it was the arrangement. *Why* did you leave early? Why?"

Her hands hid her face.

"Are you still mad?" Smiley shouted. "Do you still think you can control what you have made? Freitag will kill you, kill the girl, kill, kill, kill. Who are you trying to protect, a girl or a murderer?"

She wept and said nothing. Smiley crouched beside her, still shouting.

"I'll tell you why you left early, shall I? I'll tell you what I think. It was to catch the last post that night from Weybridge. He hadn't come, you hadn't exchanged cloakroom tickets, had you, so you obeyed the instructions, you posted your ticket to him and you *have* got an address, not written down but remembered, remembered forever: 'If there is a crisis, if I do not come, this is the address': is that what he said? An address never to be used or spoken of, an address forgotten and remembered for ever? Is that right? Tell me!"

She stood up, her head turned away, went to the desk

and found a piece of paper and a pencil. The tears still ran freely over her face. With agonising slowness she wrote the address, her hand faltering and almost stopping between the words.

He took the paper from her, folded it carefully across the middle and put it in his wallet.

Now he would make her some tea.

She looked like a child rescued from the sea. She sat on the edge of the sofa holding the cup tightly in her frail hands, nursing it against her body. Her thin shoulders were hunched forward, her feet and ankles pressed tightly together. Smiley, looking at her, felt he had broken something he should never have touched because it was so fragile. He felt an obscene, coarse bully, his offerings of tea a futile recompense for his clumsiness.

He could think of nothing to say. After a while, she said: "He liked you, you know. He really liked you . . . he said you were a clever little man. It was quite a surprise when Samuel called anyone clever." She shook her head slowly. Perhaps it was the reaction that made her smile: "He used to say there were two forces in the world, the positive and the negative. 'What shall I do then?' he would ask me; 'Let them ruin their harvest because they give me bread? Creation, progress, power, the whole future of mankind waits at their door: shall I not let them in?' And I said to him: 'but Samuel, maybe the people are happy without these things?' But you know he didn't think of people like that.

"But I couldn't stop him. You know the strangest thing about Fennan? For all that thinking and talking, he had made up his mind long ago what he would do. All the rest was poetry. He wasn't co-ordinated, that's what I used to tell him . . ."

". . . and yet you helped him," said Smiley.

"Yes, I helped him. He wanted help so I gave it him. He was my life."

"I see."

"That was a mistake. He was a little boy, you know. He forgot things just like a child. And so vain. He had made up his mind to do it and he did it so badly. He

98

didn't think of it as you do, or I do. He simply didn't think of it like that. It was his work and that was all.

"It began so simply. He brought home a draft telegram one night and showed it to me. He said; 'I think Dieter ought to see that'—that was all. I couldn't believe it to begin with—that he was a spy, I mean. Because he was, wasn't he? And gradually, I realised. They began to ask for special things. The music case I got back from Freitag began to contain orders, and sometimes money. I said to him: 'Look at what they are sending you—do you want this?' We didn't know what to do with the money. In the end we gave it away mostly, I don't know why. Dieter was very angry that winter, when I told him."

"What winter was that?" asked Smiley.

"The second winter with Dieter—1956 in Mürren. We met him first in January, 1955. That was when it began. And shall I tell you something? Hungary made no difference to Samuel, not a tiny bit of difference. Dieter was frightened about him then, I know, because Freitag told me. When Fennan gave me the things to take to Weybridge that November I nearly went mad. I shouted at him: 'Can't you see it's the same? The same guns, the same children dying in the streets? Only the dream has changed, the blood is the same colour. Is this what you want?' I asked him: 'Would you do this for Germans, too? It's me who lies in the gutter, will you let them do it to *me*?' But he just said: 'No Elsa, this is different.' And I went on taking the music case. Do you understand?"

"I don't know. I just don't know. I think perhaps I do."

"He was all I had. He was my life. I protected myself, I suppose. And gradually I became a part of it, and then it was too late to stop. . . . And then you know," she said, in a whisper; "there were times when I was glad, times when the world seemed to applaud what Samuel was doing. It was not a pretty sight for us, the new Germany. Old names had come back, names that had frightened us as children. The dreadful, plump

99

pride returned, you could see it even in the photographs in the papers, they marched with the old rhythm. Fennan felt that too, but then thank God he hadn't seen what I saw.

"We were in a camp outside Dresden, where we used to live. My father was paralysed. He missed tobacco more than anything and I used to roll cigarettes from any rubbish I could find in the camp—just to pretend with. One day a guard saw him smoking and began laughing. Some others came and they laughed too. My father was holding the cigarette in his paralysed hand and it was burning his fingers. He didn't know, you see.

"Yes, when they gave guns to the Germans again, gave them money and uniforms, then sometimes—just for a little while—I was pleased with what Samuel had done. We are Jews, you know, and so . . ."

"Yes, I know, I understand," said Smiley: "I saw it too, a little of it."

"Dieter said you had."

"Dieter said that?"

"Yes. To Freitag. He told Freitag you were a very clever man. You once deceived Dieter before the war, and it was only long afterwards that he found out, that's what Freitag said. He said you were the best he'd ever met."

"When did Freitag tell you that?"

She looked at him for a long time. He had never seen in any face such hopeless misery. He remembered how she had said to him before; "The children of my grief are dead." He understood that now, and heard it in her voice when at last she spoke:

"Why, isn't it obvious? The night he murdered Samuel.

"That's the great joke, Mr. Smiley. At the very moment when Samuel could have done so much for them—not just a piece here and a piece there, but all the time—so many music cases—at that moment their own fear destroyed them, turned them into animals and made them kill what they had made.

"Samuel always said; 'they will win because they *know* and the others will perish because they do not: men who work for a dream will work for ever'—that's what he said. But I knew their dream, I knew it would destroy us. What has not destroyed? Even the dream of Christ."

"It was Dieter then, who saw me in the park with Fennan?"

"Yes."

"And thought—"

"Yes. Thought that Samuel had betrayed him. Told Freitag to kill Samuel."

"And the anonymous letter?"

"I don't know. I don't know who wrote it. Someone who knew Samuel I suppose, someone from the office who watched him and knew. Or from Oxford, from the Party. I don't know. Samuel didn't know either."

"But the suicide letter—"

She looked at him, and her face crumpled. She was almost weeping again. She bowed her head:

"I wrote it. Freitag brought the paper, and I wrote it. The signature was already there. Samuel's signature."

Smiley went over to her, sat beside her on the sofa and took her hand. She turned on him in a fury and began screaming at him:

"Take your hands off me! Do you think I'm yours because I don't belong to them? Go away! Go away and kill Freitag and Dieter, keep the game alive, Mr. Smiley. But don't think I'm on *your* side, d'you hear? Because I'm the wandering Jewess, the no-man's land, the battlefield for your toy soldiers. You can kick me and trample on me, see, but never, never touch me, never tell me you're sorry, d'you hear? Now get out! Go away and kill."

She sat there, shivering as if from cold. As he reached the door he looked back. There were no tears in her eyes.

Mendel was waiting for him in the car.

XIII

THE INEFFICIENCY OF
SAMUEL FENNAN

They arrived at Mitcham at lunch time. Peter Guillam
was waiting for them patiently in his car.

"Well, children; what's the news?"

Smiley handed him the piece of paper from his wallet. "There was an emergency number, too—Primrose
9747. You'd better check it but I'm not hopeful of that
either."

Peter disappeared into the hall and began telephoning. Mendel busied himself in the kitchen and returned
ten minutes later with beer, bread and cheese on a tray.
Guillam came back and sat down without saying anything. He looked worried. "Well," he said at last; "what
did she say, George?"

Mendel cleared away as Smiley finished the account
of his interview that morning.

"I see," said Guillam. "How very worrying. Well,
that's it, George, I shall have to put this on paper today,
and I'll have to go to Maston at once. Catching dead
spies is a poor game really—and causes a lot of unhap-
piness."

"What access did he have at the F.O.?" asked Smiley.

"Recently a lot. That's why they felt he should be interviewed, as you know."

"What kind of stuff, mainly?"

"I don't know yet. He was on an Asian desk until a few months ago but his new job was different."

"American, I seem to remember," said Smiley. "Peter?"

"Yes."

"Peter, have you thought at all *why* they wanted to kill Fennan so much. I mean, supposing he *had* betrayed them, as they thought, why kill him? They had nothing to gain."

"No; no, I suppose they hadn't. That does need some explaining, come to think of it . . . or does it? Suppose Fuchs or Maclean had betrayed them, I wonder what would have happened. Suppose they had reason to fear a chain reaction—not just here but in America— all over the world? Wouldn't they kill him to prevent that? There's so much we shall just never know."

"Like the 8.30 call?" said Smiley.

"Cheerio. Hang on here till I ring you, will you? Maston's bound to want to see you. They'll be running down the corridors when I tell them the glad news. I shall have to wear that special grin I reserve for bearing really disastrous tidings."

Mendel saw him out and then returned to the drawing-room. "Best thing you can do is put your feet up," he said. "You look a ruddy mess, you do."

"Either Mundt's here or he's not," thought Smiley as he lay on the bed in his waistcoat, his hands linked under his head. "If he's not, we're finished. It will be for Maston to decide what to do with Elsa Fennan, and my guess is he'll do nothing.

"If Mundt *is* here, it's for one of three reasons: A, because Dieter told him to stay and watch the dust settle; B, because he's in bad odour and afraid to go back; C, because he has unfinished business.

"A is improbable because it's not like Dieter to take needless risks. Anyway, it's a woolly idea.

"B is unlikely because, while Mundt may be afraid of Dieter he must also, presumably, be frightened of a murder charge here. His wisest plan would be to go to another country.

"C is more likely. If I was in Dieter's shoes I'd be worried sick about Elsa Fennan. The Pidgeon girl is immaterial—without Elsa to fill in the gaps she presents no serious danger. She was not a conspirator and there is no reason why she should particularly remember Elsa's friend at the theatre. No, Elsa constitutes the real danger."

There was, of course, a final possibility, which Smiley was quite unable to judge: the possibility that Dieter had other agents to control here through Mundt. On the whole he was inclined to discount this, but the thought had no doubt crossed Peter's mind.

No . . . it still didn't make sense—it wasn't tidy. He decided to begin again.

What do we know? He sat up to look for pencil and paper and at once his head began throbbing. Obstinately he got off the bed and took a pencil from the inside pocket of his jacket. There was a writing pad in his suitcase. He returned to the bed, shaped the pillows to his satisfaction, took four aspirin from the bottle on the table and propped himself against the pillows, his short legs stretched before him. He began writing. First he wrote the heading in a neat, scholarly hand, and underlined it.

"What do we know?"

Then he began, stage by stage, to recount as dispassionately as possible the sequence of events hitherto:

"On Monday 2nd January Dieter Frey saw me in the park talking to his agent and concluded . . ." Yes, what *did* Dieter conclude? That Fennan had confessed, was going to confess? That Fennan was *my* agent? ". . .

and concluded that Fennan was dangerous, for reasons still unknown. The following evening, the first Tuesday in the month, Elsa Fennan took her husband's reports in a music case to the Weybridge Repertory Theatre, in the agreed way, and left the case in the cloakroom in exchange for a ticket. Mundt was to bring his own music case and do the same thing. Elsa and Mundt would then exchange tickets during the performance. Mundt did not appear. Accordingly she followed the emergency procedure and posted the ticket to a prearranged address, having left the theatre early to catch the last post from Weybridge. She then drove home to be met by Mundt, who had, by then, murdered Fennan, probably on Dieter's orders. He had shot him at point blank range as soon as he met him in the hall. Knowing Dieter, I suspect that he had long ago taken the precaution of keeping in London a few sheets of blank writing paper signed with samples, forged or authentic, of Sam Fennan's signature, in case it was ever necessary to compromise or blackmail him. Assuming this to be so, Mundt brought a sheet with him in order to type the suicide letter over the signature on Fennan's own typewriter. In the ghastly scene which must have followed Elsa's arrival, Mundt realised that Dieter had wrongly interpreted Fennan's encounter with Smiley, but relied on Elsa to preserve her dead husband's reputation—not to mention her own complicity. Mundt was therefore reasonably safe. Mundt made Elsa type the letter, perhaps because he did not trust his English. (Note: But who the devil typed the *first* letter, the denunciation?)

"Mundt then, presumably, demanded the music case he had failed to collect, and Elsa told him that she had obeyed standing instructions and posted the cloakroom ticket to the Hampstead address, leaving the music case at the theatre. Mundt reacted significantly: he forced her to telephone the theatre and to arrange for him to collect the case that night on his way back to London. Therefore either the address to which the ticket was posted was no longer valid, or Mundt intended at that stage to return home early the next morning without having time to collect the ticket and the case.

"Smiley visits Walliston early on the morning of Wednesday 4th January and during the *first* interview takes an 8.30 call from the exchange which (beyond reasonable doubt) Fennan requested at 7.55 the previous evening. Why?

"Later that morning S. returns to Elsa Fennan to ask about the 8.30 call—which she knew (on her own admission) would 'worry me' (no doubt Mundt's flattering description of my powers had had its effect). Having told S. a futile story about her bad memory she panics and rings Mundt.

"Mundt, presumably equipped with a photograph or a description from Dieter, decides to liquidate S. (on Dieter's authority?) and later that day nearly succeeds. (Note: Mundt did not return the car to Scarr's garage till the night of the 4th. This does not necessarily prove that Mundt had no plans for flying earlier in the day. If he had originally meant to fly in the morning he might well have left the car at Scarr's earlier and gone to the airport by bus.)

"It does seem pretty likely that Mundt changed his plans after Elsa's telephone call. It is not clear that he changed them *because of* her call." Would Mundt really be panicked by Elsa? Panicked into staying, panicked into murdering Adam Scarr, he wondered.

The telephone was ringing in the hall . . .

"George, it's Peter. No joy with the address or the telephone number. Dead end."

"What do you mean?"

. "The telephone number and the address both led to the same place—furnished apartment in Highgate village."

"Well?"

"Rented by a pilot in Lufteuropa. He paid his two months' rent on 5th January and hasn't come back since."

"Damn."

"The landlady remembers Mundt quite well. The pilot's friend. A nice polite gentleman he was, for a German, very open handed. He used to sleep on the sofa quite often."

"Oh God."

"I went through the room with a toothcomb. There was a desk in the corner. All the drawers were empty except one, which contained a cloakroom ticket. I wonder where that came from . . . Well, if you want a laugh, come round to the Circus. The whole of Olympus is seething with activity. Oh, incidentally—"

"Yes?"

"I dug around at Dieter's flat. Another lemon. He left on 4th January. Didn't tell the milkman."

"What about his mail?"

"He never received any, apart from bills. I also had a look at Comrade Mundt's little nest: couple of rooms over the Steel Mission. The furniture went out with the rest of the stuff. Sorry."

"I see."

"I'll tell you an odd thing though, George. You remember I thought I might get on to Fennan's personal possessions—wallet, note-book and so on? From the police."

"Yes."

"Well, I did. His diary's got Dieter's full name entered in the address section with the Mission telephone number against it. Bloody cheek."

"It's more than that. It's lunacy. Good Lord."

"Then for the fourth of January the entry is 'Smiley C.A. Ring 8.30.' That was corroborated by an entry for the third, which ran 'request call for Wed. morning.' There's your mysterious call."

"Still unexplained." A pause.

"George, I sent Felix Taverner round to the F.O. to do some ferreting. It's worse than we feared in one way, but better in another."

"Why?"

"Well, Taverner got his hands on the registry sched-

ules for the last two years. He was able to work out
what files have been marked to Fennan's section.
Where a file was particularly requested by that section
they still have a requisition form."

"I'm listening."

"Felix found that three or four files were usually
marked in to Fennan on a Friday afternoon and marked
out again on Monday morning; the inference is that he
took the stuff home at week-ends."

"Oh my Lord!"

"But the odd thing is, George, that during the last six
months, since his posting in fact, he tended to take
home *unclassified* stuff which wouldn't have been of interest to anyone."

"But it was during the last months that he began
dealing mainly with secret files," said Smiley. "He could
take home anything he wanted."

"I know, but he didn't. In fact you'd almost say it
was deliberate. He took home very low-grade stuff
barely related to his daily work. His colleagues can't understand it now they think about it—he even took back
some files handling subjects outside the scope of his
section."

"And unclassified."

"Yes—of no conceivable intelligence value."

"How about earlier, before he came into his new job?
What kind of stuff went home then?"

"Much more what you'd expect—files he'd used during the day, policy and so on."

"Secret?"

"Some were, some weren't. As they came."

"But nothing unexpected—no particularly delicate
stuff that didn't concern him?"

"No. Nothing. He had opportunity galore quite
frankly and didn't use it. Windy, I suppose."

"So he ought to be if he puts his controller's name in
his diary."

"And make what you like of this: he'd arranged at
the F.O. to take a day off on the fourth—the day after

he died. Rather an event apparently—he was a glutton for work, they say."

"What's Maston doing about all this?" asked Smiley, after a pause.

"Going through the files at the moment and rushing in to see me with bloody fool questions every two minutes. I think he gets lonely in there with hard facts."

"Oh, he'll beat them down, Peter, don't worry."

"He's already saying that the whole case against Fennan rests on the evidence of a neurotic woman."

"Thanks for ringing, Peter."

"Be seeing you, dear boy. Keep your head down."

Smiley replaced the receiver and wondered where Mendel was. There was an evening paper on the hall table, and he glanced vaguely at the headline "Lynching: World Jewry Protests" and beneath it the account of the lynching of a Jewish shopkeeper in Düsseldorf. He opened the drawing-room door—Mendel was not there. Then he caught sight of him through the window wearing his gardening hat, hacking savagely with a pick-axe at a tree stump in the front garden. Smiley watched him for a moment, then went upstairs again to rest. As he reached the top of the stairs the telephone began ringing again.

"George—sorry to bother you again. It's about Mundt."

"Yes?"

"Flew to Berlin last night by B.E.A. Travelled under another name but was easily identified by the air hostess. That seems to be that. Hard luck, chum."

Smiley pressed down the cradle with his hand for a moment, then dialled Walliston 2944. He heard the number ringing the other end. Suddenly the dialling tone stopped and instead he heard Elsa Fennan's voice:

"Hullo . . . Hullo . . . *Hullo?*"

Slowly he replaced the receiver. She was alive.

Why on earth *now?* Why should Mundt go home *now,* five weeks after murdering Fennan, three weeks after murdering Scarr; why had he eliminated the lesser danger—Scarr—and left Elsa Fennan unharmed, neurotic and embittered, liable at any moment to throw aside her own safety and tell the whole story? What effect might that terrible night not have had upon her? How could Dieter trust a woman now so lightly bound to him? Her husband's good name could no longer be preserved; might she not, in God knows what mood of vengeance or repentance, blurt out the whole truth? Obviously, a little time must elapse between the murder of Fennan and the murder of his wife, but what event, what information, what danger, had decided Mundt to return last night? A ruthless and elaborate plan to preserve the secrecy of Fennan's treason had now apparently been thrown aside unfinished. What had happened yesterday that Mundt could know of? Or was the timing of his departure a coincidence? Smiley refused to believe it was. If Mundt had remained in England after the two murders and the assault on Smiley, he had done so unwillingly, waiting upon some opportunity or event that would release him. He would not stay a moment longer than he need. Yet what had he done since Scarr's death? Hidden in some lonely room, locked away from light and news. Then why did he now fly home so suddenly?

And Fennan—what spy was this who selected innocuous information for his masters when he had such gems at his fingertips? A change of heart, perhaps? A weakening of purpose? Then why did he not tell his wife, for whom his crime was a constant nightmare, who would have rejoiced at his conversion? It seemed now that Fennan had never shown any preference for secret papers—he had simply taken home whatever files currently might occupy him. But certainly a weakening of purpose would explain the strange summons to Marlow and Dieter's conviction that Fennan was betraying him. And who wrote the anonymous letter?

Nothing made sense, nothing. Fennan himself—brilliant, fluent and attractive—had deceived so naturally, so expertly. Smiley had really liked him. Why then had this practised deceiver made the incredible blunder of putting Dieter's name in his diary—and shown so little judgement or interest in the selection of intelligence?

Smiley went upstairs to pack the few possessions which Mendel had collected for him from Bywater Street. It was all over.

XIV

THE DRESDEN GROUP

He stood on the doorstep and put down his suitcase, fumbling for his latchkey. As he opened the door he recalled how Mundt had stood there looking at him, those very pale blue eyes calculating and steady. It was odd to think of Mundt as Dieter's pupil. Mundt had proceeded with the inflexibility of a trained mercenary—efficient, purposeful, narrow. There had been nothing original in his technique: in everything he had been a shadow of his master. It was as if Dieter's brilliant and imaginative tricks had been compressed into a manual which Mundt had learnt by heart, adding only the salt of his own brutality.

Smiley had deliberately left no forwarding address and a heap of mail lay on the door mat. He picked it up, put it on the hall table and began opening doors and peering about him, a puzzled, lost expression on his face. The house was strange to him, cold and musty. As he moved slowly from one room to another he began for the first time to realise how empty his life had become.

He looked for matches to light the gas fire, but there were none. He sat in an armchair in the living-room and his eyes wandered over the bookshelves and the

112

odds and ends he had collected on his travels. When Ann had left him he had begun by rigorously excluding all trace of her. He had even got rid of her books. But gradually he had allowed the few remaining symbols that linked his life with hers to reassert themselves: wedding presents from close friends which had meant too much to be given away. There was a Watteau sketch from Peter Guillam, a Dresden group from Steed-Asprey.

He got up from his chair and went over to the corner cupboard where the group stood. He loved to admire the beauty of those figures, the tiny rococo courtesan in shepherd's costume, her hands outstretched to one adoring lover, her little face bestowing glances on another. He felt inadequate before that fragile perfection, as he had felt before Ann when he first began the conquest which had amazed society. Somehow those little figures comforted him: it was as useless to expect fidelity of Ann as of this tiny shepherdess in her glass case. Steed-Asprey had bought the group in Dresden before the war, it had been the prize of his collection and he had given it to them. Perhaps he had guessed that one day Smiley might have need of the simple philosophy it propounded.

Dresden: of all German cities, Smiley's favourite. He had loved its architecture, its odd jumble of mediaeval and classical buildings, sometimes reminiscent of Oxford, its cupolas, towers and spires, its copper-green roofs shimmering under a hot sun. Its name meant "town of the forest-dwellers" and it was there that Wenceslas of Bohemia had favored the minstrel poets with gifts and privilege. Smiley remembered the last time he had been there, visiting a University acquaintance, a Professor of Philology he had met in England. It was on that visit that he had caught sight of Dieter Frey, struggling round the prison courtyard. He could see him still, tall and angry, monstrously altered by his shaven head, somehow too big for that little prison. Dresden, he remembered, had been Elsa's birthplace. He remembered glancing through her personal particulars at the Ministry: Elsa *née* Freimann, born 1917 in Dresden, Germany, of German parents; educated Dresden; imprisoned 1938–45. He tried to place her against the background of her home, the patrician Jewish family living out its life amid insult and persecution. "I dreamed of long golden hair and they shaved my head." He realised with sickening accuracy why she dyed her hair. She might have been like this shepherdess, round-bosomed and pretty. But the body had been broken with hunger so that it was frail and ugly, like the carcass of a tiny bird.

He could picture her on the terrible night when she found her husband's murderer standing by his body: hear her breathless, sobbing explanation of why Fennan had been in the park with Smiley: and Mundt unmoved, explaining and reasoning, compelling her finally to conspire once more against her will in this most dreadful and needless of crimes, dragging her to the telephone and forcing her to ring the theatre, leaving her finally tortured and exhausted to cope with the enquiries that were bound to follow, even to type that futile suicide letter over Fennan's signature. It was inhuman beyond belief and, he added to himself, for Mundt a fantastic risk.

She had, of course, proved herself a reliable enough accomplice in the past, cool-headed and, ironically, more skilful than Fennan in the techniques of espionage. And, heaven knows, for a woman who had been through such a night as that, her performance at their first meeting had been a marvel.

As he stood gazing at the little shepherdess, poised eternally between her two admirers, he realised dispassionately that there was another quite different solution to the case of Samuel Fennan, a solution which matched every detail of circumstance, reconciled the nagging inconsistencies apparent in Fennan's character. The realisation began as an academic exercise without reference to personalities; Smiley manoeuvred the characters like pieces in a puzzle, twisting them this way and that to fit the complex framework of established facts—and then, in a moment, the pattern had suddenly reformed with such assurance that it was a game no more.

His heart beat faster, as with growing astonishment Smiley retold to himself the whole story, reconstructed scenes and incidents in the light of his discovery. Now he knew why Mundt had left England that day, why Fennan chose so little that was of value to Dieter, had asked for the 8.30 call, and why his wife had escaped the systematic savagery of Mundt. Now at last he knew who had written the anonymous letter. He saw how he had been the fool of his own sentiment, had played false with the power of his mind.

He went to the telephone and dialled Mendel's number. As soon as he had finished speaking to him he rang Peter Guillam. Then he put on his hat and coat and walked round the corner to Sloane Square. At a small newsagent's beside Peter Jones he bought a picture postcard of Westminster Abbey. He made his way to the underground station and travelled north to Highgate, where he got out. At the main post office he bought a stamp and addressed the postcard in stiff, continental capitals to Elsa Fennan. In the panel for correspondence he wrote in spiky longhand: "Wish you were here." He posted the card and noted the time, after which he returned to Sloane Square. There was nothing more he could do.

He slept soundly that night, rose early the following morning, a Saturday, and walked round the corner to buy croissants and coffee beans. He made a lot of coffee and sat in the kitchen reading *The Times* and eating his breakfast. He felt curiously calm and when the telephone rang at last he folded his paper carefully together before going upstairs to answer it.

"George, it's Peter"—the voice was urgent, almost triumphant: "George, she's bitten, I swear she has!"

"What happened?"

"The post arrived at exactly 8.35. By 9.30 she was walking briskly down the drive, booted and spurred. She made straight for the railway station and caught the

9.52 to Victoria. I put Mendel on the train and sped up by car, but I was too late to meet the train this end."

"How will you make contact with Mendel again?"

"I gave him the number of the Grosvenor Hotel and I'm there now. He's going to ring me as soon as he gets a chance and I'll join him wherever he is."

"Peter, you're taking this gently, aren't you?"

"Gentle as the wind, dear boy. I think she's losing her head. Moving like a greyhound."

Smiley rang off. He picked up his *Times* and began studying the theatre column. He must be right . . . he must be.

After that the morning passed with agonising slowness. Sometimes he would stand at the window, his hands in his pockets, watching leggy Kensington girls going shopping with beautiful young men in pale blue pullovers, or the car-cleaning brigade toiling happily in front of their houses, then drifting away to talk motoring shop and finally setting off purposefully down the road for the first pint of the week-end.

At last, after what seemed an interminable delay, the front-door bell rang and Mendel and Guillam came in, grinning cheerfully, ravenously hungry.

"Hook, line and sinker," said Guillam. "But let Mendel tell you—he did most of the dirty work. I just got in for the kill."

Mendel recounted his story precisely and accurately, looking at the ground a few feet in front of him, his thin head slightly on one side.

"She caught the 9.52 to Victoria. I kept well clear of her on the train and picked her up as she went through the barrier. Then she took a taxi to Hammersmith."

"A taxi?" Smiley interjected. "She must be out of her mind."

"She's rattled. She walks fast for a woman anyway, mind, but she damn nearly ran going down the platform. Got out at the Broadway and walked to the Sheridan Theatre. Tried the doors to the box office but they

116

were locked. She hesitated a moment then turned back and went to a café a hundred yards down the road. Ordered coffee and paid for it at once. About forty minutes later she went back to the Sheridan. The box office was open and I ducked in behind her and joined the queue. She bought two rear stalls for next Thursday, Row T, 27 and 28. When she got outside the theatre she put one ticket in an envelope and sealed it up. Then she posted it. I couldn't see the address but there was a sixpenny stamp on the envelope."

Smiley sat very still. "I wonder," he said; "I wonder if he'll come."

"I caught up with Mendel at the Sheridan," said Guillam. "He saw her into the café and then rang me. After that he went in after her."

"Felt like a coffee myself," Mendel went on. "Mr. Guillam joined me. I left him there when I joined the ticket queue, and he drifted out of the café a bit later. It was a decent job and no worries. She's rattled, I'm sure. But not suspicious."

"What did she do after that?" asked Smiley.

"Went straight back to Victoria. We left her to it."

They were silent for a moment, then Mendel said:

"What do we do now?"

Smiley blinked and gazed earnestly into Mendel's grey face.

"Book tickets for Thursday's performance at the Sheridan."

They were gone and he was alone again. He still had not begun to cope with the quantity of mail which had accumulated in his absence. Circulars, catalogues from Blackwells, bills and the usual collection of soap vouchers, frozen pea coupons, football pool forms and a few private letters still lay unopened on the hall table. He took them into the drawing-room, settled in an armchair and began opening the personal letters first. There was one from Maston, and he read it with something approaching embarrassment.

"My dear George,

I was so sorry to hear from Guillam about your accident, and I do hope that by now you have made a full recovery.

You may recall that in the heat of the moment you wrote me a letter of resignation before your misfortune, and I just wanted to let you know that I am not, of course, taking this seriously. Sometimes when events crowd in upon us our sense of perspective suffers. But old campaigners like ourselves, George, are not so easily put off the scent. I look forward to seeing you with us again as soon as you are strong enough, and in the meantime we continue to regard you as an old and loyal member of the staff."

Smiley put this on one side and turned to the next letter. Just for a moment he did not recognise the handwriting; just for a moment he looked bleakly at the Swiss stamp and the expensive hotel writing paper. Suddenly he felt slightly sick, his vision blurred and there was scarcely strength enough in his fingers to tear open the envelope. What did she want? If money, she could have all he possessed. The money was his own, to spend as he wished; if it gave him pleasure to squander it on Ann, he would do so. There was nothing else he had to give her—she had taken it long ago. Taken his courage, his love, his compassion, carried them jauntily away in her little jewel case to fondle occasionally on odd afternoons when the time hung heavy in the Cuban sun, to dangle them perhaps before the eyes of her newest lover, to compare them even with similar trinkets which others before or since had brought her.

"My darling George,

I want to make you an offer which no gentleman could accept. I want to come back to you.

I'm staying at the Baur-au-Lac at Zurich till the end of the month. Let me know.

Ann."

Smiley picked up the envelope and looked at the back of it: "Madame Juan Alvida." No, no gentleman could accept that offer. No dream could survive the daylight of Ann's departure with her saccharine Latin and his orange-peel grin. Smiley had once seen a news film of Alvida winning some race in Monte Carlo. The most repellent thing about him, he remembered, had been the hair on his arms. With his goggles and the motor oil and that ludicrous laurel-wreath he had looked exactly like an anthropoid ape fallen from a tree. He was wearing a white tennis shirt with short sleeves, which had somehow remained spotlessly clean throughout the race, setting off those black monkey arms with repulsive clarity.

That was Ann: Let me know. Redeem your life, see whether it can be lived again and let me know. I have wearied my lover, my lover has wearied me, let me shatter your world again: my own bores me. I want to come back to you . . . I want, I want . . .

Smiley got up, the letter still in his hand and stood again before the porcelain group. He remained there several minutes, gazing at the little shepherdess. She was so beautiful.

XV

THE LAST ACT

The Sheridan's three-act production of "Edward II" was playing to a full house. Guillam and Mendel sat in adjacent seats at the extreme end of the circle, which formed a wide U facing the stage. The left-hand end of the circle afforded a view of the rear stalls, which were otherwise concealed. An empty seat separated Guillam from a party of young students buzzing with anticipation.

They looked down thoughtfully on a restless sea of bobbing heads and fluttering programmes, stirring in sudden waves as later arrivals took their places. The scene reminded Guillam of an Oriental dance, where the tiny gestures of hand and foot animate a motionless body. Occasionally he would glance towards the rear stalls, but there was still no sign of Elsa Fennan or her guest.

Just as the recorded overture was ending he looked again briefly towards the two empty stalls in the back row and his heart gave a sudden leap as he saw the slight figure of Elsa Fennan sitting straight and motionless, staring fixedly down the auditorium like a child learning deportment. The seat on her right, nearest the gangway, was still empty.

Outside in the street taxis were drawing up hastily at the theatre entrance and an agreeable selection of the established and the disestablished hurriedly over-tipped their cabmen and spent five minutes looking for their tickets. Smiley's taxi took him past the theatre and deposited him at the Clarendon Hotel, where he went straight downstairs to the dining-room and bar.

"I'm expecting a call any moment," he said. "My name's Savage. You'll let me know, won't you?"

The barman turned to the telephone behind him and spoke to the receptionist.

"And a small whisky and soda, please; will you have one yourself?"

"Thank you sir, I never touch it."

The curtain rose on a dimly lit stage and Guillam, peering towards the back of the auditorium, tried at first without success to penetrate the sudden darkness. Gradually his eyes accustomed themselves to the faint glow cast by the emergency lamps, until he could just discern Elsa in the half light; and still the empty seat beside her.

Only a low partition separated the rear stalls from the gangway which ran along the back of the auditorium, and behind it were several doors leading to the foyer, bar and cloakrooms. For a brief moment one of these opened and an oblique shaft of light was cast as if by design upon Elsa Fennan, illuminating with a thin line one side of her face, making its hollows black by contrast. She inclined her head slightly, as if listening to something behind her, half rose in her seat, then sat down again, deceived, and resumed her former attitude.

Guillam felt Mendel's hand on his arm, turned, and saw his lean face thrust forward, looking past him. Following Mendel's gaze, he peered down into the well of the theatre, where a tall figure was slowly making his way towards the back of the stalls; he was an impressive sight, erect and handsome, a lock of black hair tumbling over his brow. It was he whom Mendel watched with such fascination, this elegant giant limping up the gangway. There was something different about him, something arresting and disturbing. Through his glasses Guillam watched his slow and deliberate progress, admired the grace and measure of his uneven walk. He was a man apart, a man you remember, a man who strikes a chord deep in your experience, a man with the gift of universal familiarity: to Guillam he was a living component of all our romantic dreams, he stood at the mast with Conrad, sought the lost Greece with Byron and with Goethe visited the shades of classical and mediaeval hells.

As he walked, thrusting his good leg forward, there was a defiance, a command, that could not go unheeded. Guillam noticed how heads turned in the audience, and eyes followed him obediently.

Pushing past Mendel, Guillam stepped quickly through the emergency exit into the corridor behind. He followed the corridor down some steps and arrived at last at the foyer. The box office had closed down, but the girl was still poring hopelessly over a page of laboriously compiled figures, covered with alterations and erasions.

"Excuse me," said Guillam; "but I must use your telephone—it's urgent, do you mind?"

"Ssh!" She waved a pencil at him impatiently, without looking up. Her hair was mousy, her oily skin glistened from the fatigue of late nights and a diet of chipped potatoes. Guillam waited a moment, wondering how long it would be before she found a solution to that tangle of spidery numerals which would match the pile of notes and silver in the open cash box beside her.

"Listen," he urged; "I'm a police officer—there's a couple of heroes upstairs who are after your cash. Now will you let me use that telephone?"

"Oh Lord," she said in a tired voice, and looked at him for the first time. She wore glasses and was very plain. She was neither alarmed nor impressed; "I wish they'd perishing well take the money. It sends me up the wall." Pushing her accounts to one side she opened a door beside the little kiosk and Guillam squeezed in.

"Hardly decent, is it?" the girl said with a grin. Her voice was nearly cultured—probably a London undergraduate earning pin-money, thought Guillam. He rang the Clarendon and asked for Mr. Savage. Almost immediately he heard Smiley's voice.

"He's here," said Guillam, "been here all the time. Must have bought an extra ticket; he was sitting in the front stalls. Mendel suddenly spotted him limping up the aisle."

"Limping?"

"Yes, it's not Mundt. It's the other one. Dieter."

Smiley did not reply and after a moment Guillam said: "George—are you there?"

"We've had it I'm afraid, Peter. We've got nothing against Frey. Call the men off, they won't find Mundt tonight. Is the first act over yet?"

"Must be just coming up for the interval."

"I'll be round in twenty minutes. Hang on to Elsa like grim death—if they leave and separate Mendel's to stick to Dieter. You stay in the foyer for the last act in case they leave early."

Guillam replaced the receiver and turned to the girl. "Thanks," he said, and put four pennies on her desk. She hastily gathered them together and pressed them firmly into his hand.

"For God's sake," she said; "don't add to my troubles."

He went outside into the street and spoke to a plain clothes man loitering on the pavement. Then he hurried back and rejoined Mendel as the curtain fell on the first act.

Elsa and Dieter were sitting side by side. They were talking happily together, Dieter laughing, Elsa animated and articulate like a puppet brought to life by her master. Mendel watched them in fascination. She laughed at something Dieter said, leant forward and put her hand on his arm. He saw her thin fingers against his dinner jacket, saw Dieter incline his head and whisper something to her, so that she laughed again. As Mendel watched, the theatre lights dimmed and the noise of conversation subsided as the audience quickly prepared for the second act.

Smiley left the Clarendon and walked slowly along the pavement towards the theatre. Thinking about it now, he realised that it was logical enough that Dieter should come, that it would have been madness to send Mundt. He wondered how long it could be before Elsa and Dieter discovered that it was not Dieter who had summoned her, not Dieter who had sent the postcard by a trusted courier. That, he reflected, should be an interesting moment. All he prayed for now was the opportunity of one more interview with Elsa Fennan.

A few minutes later he slipped quietly into the empty seat beside Guillam. It was a long time since he had seen Dieter.

He had not changed. He was the same improbable romantic with the magic of a charlatan; the same unforgettable figure which had struggled over the ruins of Germany, implacable of purpose, satanic in fulfilment, dark and swift like the Gods of the North. Smiley had lied to them that night in his club; Dieter *was* out of proportion, his cunning, his conceit, his strength and his dream—all were larger than life, undiminished by the moderating influence of experience. He was a man who thought and acted in absolute terms, without patience or compromise.

Memories returned to Smiley that night as he sat in the dark theatre and watched Dieter across a mass of motionless faces, memories of dangers shared, of mutual trust when each had held in his hand the life of the other. . . . Just for a second Smiley wondered whether Dieter had seen him, had the feeling that Dieter's eyes were upon him, watching him in the dim half light.

Smiley got up as the second act drew to a close; as the curtain fell he made quickly for the side exit and waited discreetly in the corridor until the bell rang for the last act. Mendel joined him shortly before the end of the interval, and Guillam slipped past them to take up his post in the foyer.

"There's trouble," Mendel said. "They're arguing. She looks frightened. She keeps on saying something and he just shakes his head. She's panicking I think, and Dieter looks worried. He's started looking round the theatre as if he was trapped, getting the measure of the place, making plans. He glanced up to where you'd been sitting."

"He won't let her leave alone," said Smiley. "He'll wait and get out with the crowd. They won't leave before the end. He probably reckons he's surrounded: he'll bargain on flustering us by parting from her suddenly in the middle of a crowd—just losing her."

"What's our game? Why can't we go down there and get them?"

"We just wait; I don't know what for. We've no proof. No proof of murder and none of espionage until Maston decides to do something. But remember this: Dieter doesn't know that. If Elsa's jumpy and Dieter's worried, they'll do *something*—that's certain. So long as *they* think the game is up, we've a chance. Let them bolt, panic, anything. So long as they do something. . . ."

It was dark in the theatre again, but out of the corner of his eye Smiley saw Dieter leaning over Elsa whispering to her. His left hand held her arm, his whole attitude was one of urgent persuasion and reassurance.

The play dragged on, the shouts of soldiers and the screams of the demented king filled the theatre, until the dreadful climax of his foul death, when an audible sigh rose from the stalls beneath them. Dieter had his arm round Elsa's shoulders now, he had gathered the folds of her thin wrap about her neck and protected her as if she were a sleeping child. They remained like this until the final curtain. Neither applauded. Dieter looked about for Elsa's handbag, said something reassuring to her and put it on her lap. She nodded very slightly. A warning roll of the drums brought the audience to its feet for the national anthem—Smiley rose instinctively and noticed to his surprise that Mendel had vanished.

Dieter slowly stood up and as he did so Smiley realised that something had happened. Elsa was still sitting and though Dieter gently prevailed on her to rise, she made no answering sign. There was something oddly dislocated in the way she sat, in the way her head lolled forward on her shoulders. . . .

The last line of the anthem was beginning as Smiley rushed to the door, ran down the corridor, down the stone stairs to the foyer. He was just too late—he was met by the first crowd of anxious theatre-goers hastening towards the street in search of taxis. He looked wildly among the crowd for Dieter and knew it was hopeless—that Dieter had done what he himself would have done, had chosen one of the dozen emergency exits which led to the street and safety. He pushed his bulky frame gradually through the middle of the crowd towards the entrance to the stalls. As he twisted this way and that, forcing himself between oncoming bodies, he caught sight of Guillam at the edge of the stream searching hopelessly for Dieter and Elsa. He shouted to him, and Guillam turned quickly.

Struggling on, Smiley at last found himself against the low partition and he could see Elsa Fennan sitting motionless as all around her men stood up and women felt for their coats and handbags. Then he heard the scream. It was sudden, short and utterly expressive of horror and disgust. A girl was standing in the gangway looking at Elsa. She was young and very pretty, the fingers of her right hand were raised to her mouth, her face was deathly white. Her father, a tall cadaverous man, stood behind her. He grasped her shoulders quickly and drew her back as he caught sight of the dreadful thing before him.

Elsa's wrap had slipped from her shoulders and her head was lolling on to her chest.

Smiley had been right. "Let them bolt, panic, anything . . . so long as they do *something* . . ." And this was what they had done: this broken, wretched body was witness to their panic.

"You'd better get the police, Peter. I'm going home.

Keep me out of it, if you can. You know where to find me." He nodded, as if to himself; "I'm going home."

It was foggy, and a fine rain was falling as Mendel quickly darted across the Fulham Palace Road in pursuit of Dieter. The headlights of cars came suddenly out of the wet mist twenty yards from him; the noise of traffic was high-pitched and nervous as it groped its uncertain way.

He had no choice but to keep close on Dieter's heels, never more than a dozen paces behind him. The pubs and cinemas had closed but the coffee bars and dance halls still attracted noisy groups crowding the pavements. As Dieter limped ahead of him Mendel staged his progression by the street lamps, watching his silhouette suddenly clarify each time it entered the next cone of light.

Dieter was walking swiftly despite his limp. As his stride lengthened his limp became more pronounced, so that he seemed to swing his left leg forward by a sudden effort of his broad shoulders.

There was a curious expression on Mendel's face, not of hatred or iron purpose but of frank distaste. To Mendel, the frills of Dieter's profession meant nothing. He saw in his quarry only the squalor of a criminal, the cowardice of a man who paid others to do his killing. When Dieter had gently disengaged himself from the audience and moved towards the side exit, Mendel saw what he had been waiting for: the stealthy act of a common criminal. It was something he expected and understood. To Mendel there was only one criminal class, from pickpocket and sneakthief to the big operator tampering with company law; they were outside the law and it was his distasteful but necessary vocation to remove them to safe keeping. This one happened to be German.

The fog grew thick and yellow. Neither of them wore a coat. Mendel wondered what Mrs. Fennan would do now. Guillam would take care of her. She hadn't even looked at Dieter when he slinked off. She was an odd one that, all skin and bones and good works by the look of her. Lived on dry toast and Bovril.

Dieter turned abruptly down a side street to the right then another to the left. They had been walking for nearly an hour and he showed no sign of slowing down. The street seemed empty: certainly Mendel could hear no other footsteps but their own, crisp and short, the echo corrupted by the fog. They were in a narrow street of Victorian houses with hastily contrived Regency style façades, heavy porches and sash windows. Mendel guessed they were somewhere near Fulham Broadway, perhaps beyond it, nearer the King's Road. Still Dieter's pace did not flag, still the crooked shadow thrust forward into the fog, confident of its path, urgent in its purpose.

As they approached a main road Mendel heard again the plaintive whine of traffic, brought almost to a standstill by the fog. Then from somewhere above them a yellow street light shed a pale glow, its outline clearly drawn like the aura of a winter sun. Dieter hesitated a moment on the kerb, then, chancing the ghostly traffic that nosed its way past them from nowhere, he crossed the road and plunged at once into one of the innumerable side streets that led, Mendel was certain, towards the river.

Mendel's clothes were soaking wet, and the thin rain ran over his face. They must be near the river now; he thought he could detect the smell of tar and coke, feel the insidious cold of the black water. Just for a moment he thought Dieter had vanished. He moved forward quickly, nearly tripped on a kerb, went forward again and saw the railings of the embankment in front of him. Steps led upwards to an iron gate in the railings and this was slightly open. He stood at the gate and peered beyond, down into the water. There was a stout wooden gangway and Mendel heard the uneven echo as Dieter, hidden by the fog, followed his strange course to the water's edge. Mendel waited, then, wary and silent, he made his way down the gangway. It was a permanent affair with heavy pine handrails on either side. Mendel reckoned it had been there some time. The low end of the gangway was joined to a long raft made of duckboard and oil-drums. Three dilapidated houseboats loomed in the fog, rocking gently on their moorings.

Noiselessly Mendel crept on to the raft, examining each of the houseboats in turn. Two were close together, connected by a plank. The third was moored some fifteen feet away, and a light was burning in her forward cabin. Mendel returned to the embankment, closing the iron gate carefully behind him.

He walked slowly down the road, still uncertain of his bearings. After about five minutes the pavement took him suddenly to the right and the ground rose gradually. He guessed he was on a bridge. He lit his cigarette lighter, and its long flame cast a glow over the stone wall on his right. He moved the lighter back and forth, and finally came upon a wet and dirty metal plate bearing the words "Battersea Bridge." He made his way back to the iron gate and stood for a moment, orientating himself exactly in the light of his knowledge.

Somewhere above him and to his right the four massive chimneys of Fulham Power Station stood hidden in the fog. To his left was Cheyne Walk with its row of smart little boats reaching to Battersea Bridge. The place where he now stood marked the dividing line between the smart and the squalid, where Cheyne Walk meets Lots Road, one of the ugliest streets in London. The southern side of this road consists of vast warehouses, wharves and mills, and the northern side presents an unbroken line of dingy houses typical of the side streets of Fulham.

It was in the shadow of the four chimneys, perhaps sixty feet from the Cheyne Walk mooring, that Dieter Frey had found a sanctuary. Yes, Mendel knew the spot well. It was only a couple of hundred yards up river from where the earthly remains of Mr. Adam Scarr had been recovered from the unyielding arms of the Thames.

XVI

ECHOES IN THE FOG

It was long after midnight when Smiley's telephone rang. He got up from the armchair in front of the gas fire and plodded upstairs to his bedroom, his right hand gripping the banisters tightly as he went. It was Peter, no doubt, or the police, and he would have to make a statement. Or even the Press. The murder had taken place just in time to catch today's papers and mercifully too late for last night's news broadcast. What would this be? "Maniac killer in theatre"? "Death-lock murder—woman named"? He hated the Press as he hated advertising and television, he hated mass-media, the relentless persuasion of the twentieth century. Everything he admired or loved had been the product of intense individualism. That was why he hated Dieter now, hated what he stood for more strongly than ever before: it was the fabulous impertinence of renouncing the individual in favour of the mass. When had mass philosophies ever brought benefit or wisdom? Dieter cared nothing for human life: dreamed only of armies of faceless men bound by their lowest common denominators; he wanted to shape the world as if it were a tree, cutting off what did not fit the regular image; for this he fashioned blank, soulless automatons like Mundt. Mundt was faceless like Dieter's army, a trained killer born of the finest killer breed.

He picked up the telephone and gave his number. It was Mendel.

"Where are you?"

"Near Chelsea Embankment. Pub called the Balloon, in Lots Road. Landlord's a chum of mine. I knocked him up. . . . Listen, Elsa's boy friend is lying up in a houseboat by Chelsea flour mill. Bloody miracle in the fog, he is. Must have found his way by Braille."

"Who?"

"Her boy friend, her escort at the theatre. Wake up, Mr. Smiley; what's eating you?"

"You followed Dieter?"

"Of course I did. That was what you told Mr. Guillam, wasn't it? He was to stick to the woman and me the man. . . . How did Mr. Guillam get on by the way? Where did Elsa get to?"

"She didn't get anywhere. She was dead when Dieter left. Mendel, are you there? Look, for God's sake, how do I find you? Where is this place, will the police know it?"

"They'll know. Tell them he's in a converted landing craft called 'Sunset Haven.' She's lying against the eastern side of Sennen Wharf, between the flour mills and Fulham Power Station. They'll know . . . but the fog's thick, mind, very thick."

"Where can I meet you?"

"Cut straight down to the river. I'll meet you where Battersea Bridge joins the north bank."

"I'll come at once, as soon as I've rung Guillam."

He had a gun somewhere, and for a moment he thought of looking for it. Then, somehow, it seemed pointless. Besides, he reflected grimly, there'd be the most frightful row if he used it. He rang Guillam at his flat and gave him Mendel's message: "And Peter, they must cover all ports and airfields; order a special watch on river traffic and seabound craft. They'll know the form."

He put on an old mackintosh and a pair of thick leather gloves and slipped quickly out into the fog.

Mendel was waiting for him by the bridge. They nodded to one another and Mendel led him quickly along the embankment, keeping close to the river wall to avoid the trees that grew along the road. Suddenly Mendel stopped, seizing Smiley by the arm in warning. They stood motionless, listening. Then Smiley heard it too, the hollow ring of footsteps on a wooden floor, irregular like the footsteps of a limping man. They heard the creak of an iron gate, the clang as it was closed, then the footsteps again, firm now upon the pavement, growing louder, coming towards them. Neither moved. Louder, nearer, then they faltered, stopped. Smiley held his breath, trying desperately at the same time to see an extra yard into the fog, to glimpse at the waiting figure he knew was there.

Then suddenly he came, rushing like a massive wild beast, bursting through them, knocking them apart like children and running on, lost again, the uneven echo fading in the distance. They turned and chased after him, Mendel in front and Smiley following as best he could, the image vivid in his mind of Dieter, gun in hand, bursting on them out of the night fog. Ahead, the shadow of Mendel turned abruptly to the right, and Smiley followed blindly. Then suddenly the rhythm had changed to the scuffle of fighting. Smiley ran forward, heard the unmistakable sound of a heavy weapon striking a human skull and then he was upon them: saw Mendel on the ground, and Dieter stooping over him, raising his arm to hit him again with the heavy butt of an automatic pistol.

Smiley was out of breath. His chest was burning from the bitter, rank fog, his mouth hot and dry, filled with a taste like blood. Somehow he summoned breath, and he shouted desperately:

"Dieter!"

Frey looked at him, nodded and said:

"*Servus,* George," and hit Mendel a hard, brutal

blow with the pistol. He got up slowly, holding the pistol downwards and using both hands to cock it.

Smiley ran at him blindly, forgetting what little skill he had ever possessed, swinging with his short arms, striking with his open hands. His head was against Dieter's chest and he pushed forward, punching Dieter's back and sides. He was mad and, discovering in himself the energy of madness, pressed Dieter back still further towards the railing of the bridge while Dieter, off balance and hindered by his weak leg, gave way. Smiley knew Dieter was hitting him, but the decisive blow never came. He was shouting at Dieter; "Swine, swine!" and as Dieter receded still further Smiley found his arms free and once more struck at his face with clumsy, childish blows. Dieter was leaning back and Smiley saw the clean curve of his throat and chin, as with all his strength he thrust his open hand upwards. His fingers closed over Dieter's jaw and mouth and he pushed further and further. Dieter's hands were at Smiley's throat, then suddenly they were clutching at his collar to save himself as he sank slowly backwards. Smiley beat frantically at his arms, and then he was held no more and Dieter was falling, falling into the swirling fog beneath the bridge, and there was silence. No shout, no splash. He was gone; offered like a human sacrifice to the London fog and the foul black river lying beneath it.

Smiley leant over the bridge, his head throbbing wildly, blood pouring from his nose, the fingers of his right hand feeling broken and useless. His gloves were gone. He looked down into the fog and could see nothing.

"Dieter!" he cried in anguish; "Dieter!"

He shouted again, but his voice choked and tears sprang to his eyes. "Oh dear God what have I done, Oh Christ, Dieter, why didn't you stop me, why didn't you hit me with the gun, why didn't you shoot?" He pressed his clenched hands to his face, tasting the salt blood in the palms mixed with the salt of his tears. He leant against the parapet and cried like a child. Somewhere

133

beneath him a cripple dragged himself through the filthy water, lost and exhausted, yielding at last to the stenching blackness till it held him and drew him down.

He woke to find Peter Guillam sitting on the end of his bed pouring out tea.

"Ah, George. Welcome home. It's two in the afternoon."

"And this morning—?"

"This morning, dear boy, you were carolling on Battersea Bridge with Comrade Mendel."

"How is he . . . Mendel, I mean?"

"Suitably ashamed of himself. Recovering fast."

"And Dieter—"

"Dead."

Guillam handed him a cup of tea and some ratafia biscuits from Fortnums.

"How long have you been here, Peter?"

"Well, we came here in a series of tactical bounds, as it were. The first was to Chelsea Hospital where they licked your wounds and gave you a fairly substantial tranquilliser. Then we came back here and I put you to bed. That was disgusting. Then I did a spot of telephoning and, so to speak, went round with a pointed stick tidying up the mess. I looked in on you now and again. Cupid and Psyche. You were either snoring like a saddleback or reciting Webster."

"God."

"Duchess of Malfi, I think it was. 'I bad thee, when I was distracted of my wits, go kill my dearest friend, and thou hast done it!' Dreadful nonsense, George, I'm afraid."

"How did the police find us—Mendel and me?"

"George, you may not know it but you were bellowing pejoratives at Dieter as if—"

"Yes, of course. You heard."

"We heard."

"What about Maston? What does Maston say about all this?"

"I think he wants to see you. I have a message from

134

him asking you to drop in as soon as you feel well enough. I don't know what he thinks about it. Nothing at all I should imagine."

"What do you mean?"

Guillam poured out more tea.

"Use your loaf, George. All three principals in this little fairy tale have now been eaten by bears. No secret information has been compromised for the last six months. Do you really think Maston wants to dwell on the details? Do you really think he is bursting to tell the Foreign Office the good tidings—and admit that we only catch spies when we trip over their dead bodies?"

The front-door bell rang and Guillam went downstairs to answer it. In some alarm Smiley heard him admit the visitor to the hall, then the subdued sound of voices, footsteps coming up the stairs. There was a knock on the door and Maston came in. He was carrying an absurdly large bunch of flowers and looked as though he had just been to a garden party. Smiley remembered it was Friday: no doubt he was going to Henley this week-end. He was grinning. He must have been grinning all the way up the stairs.

"Well, George, in the wars again!"

"Yes, I'm afraid so. Another accident."

He sat on the edge of the bed, leaning across it, one arm supporting him the other side of Smiley's legs.

There was a pause and then he said:

"You got my note, George?"

"Yes."

Another pause.

"There has been talk of a new section in the Department, George. We (your Department, that is) feel we should devote more energy to technique research, with particular application to satellite espionage. That is also the Home Office view, I'm pleased to say. Guillam has agreed to advise on terms of reference. I wondered if you'd take it on for us. Running it I mean, with the necessary promotion of course and the option of extending your service after the statutory retirement age. Our personnel people are right behind me on this."

"Thank you . . . perhaps I could think about it, may I?"

"Of course . . . of course," Maston looked slightly put out. "When will you let me know? It may be necessary to take on some new men and the question of space arises. . . . Have the week-end to think about it will you and let me know on Monday. The Secretary was quite willing for you to—"

"Yes, I'll let you know. It's very good of you."

"Not at all. Besides I am only the Adviser you know, George. This is really an internal decision. I'm just the bringer of good news, George; my usual function of errand boy."

Maston looked at Smiley hard for a moment, hesitated and then said: "I've put the Ministers in the picture . . . as far as is necessary. We discussed what action should be taken. The Home Secretary was also present."

"When was this?"

"This morning. Some very grave issues were raised. We considered a protest to the East Germans and an extradition order for this man Mundt."

"But we don't recognise East Germany."

"Precisely. That was the difficulty. It is however possible to lodge a protest with an intermediary."

"Such as Russia?"

"Such as Russia. In the event, however, certain factors militated against this. It was felt that publicity, whatever form it took, would ultimately rebound against the nation's interests. There is already considerable popular hostility in this country to the rearmament of Western Germany. It was felt that any evidence of German intrigue in Britain—whether inspired by the Russians or not—might encourage this hostility. There is, you see, no positive evidence that Frey was operating for the Russians. It might well be represented to the public that he was operating on his own account or on behalf of a united Germany."

"I see."

"So far very few people indeed are aware of the facts

at all. That is most fortunate. On behalf of the police the Home Secretary has tentatively agreed that they will do their part in playing the affair down as far as possible. . . . Now this man Mendel, what's he like. Is he trustworthy?"

Smiley hated Maston for that.

"Yes," he said.

Maston got up. "Good," he said, "good. Well, I must get along. Anything you want at all, anything I can do?"

"No, thank you. Guillam is looking after me admirably."

Maston reached the door. "Well good luck, George. Take the job if you can." He said this quickly in a subdued voice with a pretty, sidelong smile as if it meant rather a lot to him.

"Thank you for the flowers," said Smiley.

Dieter was dead, and he had killed him. The broken fingers of his right hand, the stiffness of his body and the sickening headache, the nausea of guilt, all testified to this. And Dieter had let him do it, had not fired the gun, had remembered their friendship when Smiley had not. They had fought in a cloud, in the rising stream of the river, in a clearing in a timeless forest: they had met, two friends rejoined, and fought like beasts. Dieter had remembered and Smiley had not. They had come from different hemispheres of the night, from different worlds of thought and conduct. Dieter, mercurial, absolute, had fought to build a civilisation. Smiley, rationalistic, protective, had fought to prevent him. "Oh God," said Smiley aloud, "who was then the gentleman . . ."

Laboriously he got out of bed and began to dress. He felt better standing up.

XVII

DEAR ADVISER

"Dear Adviser,

I am at last able to reply to Personnel's offer of a higher appointment in the Department. I am sorry that I have taken so long to do this, but as you know, I have not been well recently, and have also had to contend with a number of personal problems outside the scope of the Department.

As I am not entirely free of my indisposition, I feel it would be unwise for me to accept their offer. Kindly convey this decision to Personnel.

I am sure you will understand.

Yours,
George Smiley."

"Dear Peter,

I enclose a note on the Fennan case. This is the only copy. Please pass it to Maston when you have read it. I thought it would be valuable to record the events—even if they did not take place.

Ever,
George."

"The Fennan Case"

"On Monday, 2nd January, I interviewed Samuel Arthur Fennan, a senior member of the Foreign Office, in order to clarify certain allegations made against him in an anonymous letter. The interview was arranged in accordance with the customary procedure, that is to say with the consent of the F.O. We knew of nothing adverse to Fennan beyond communist sympathy while at Oxford in the thirties, to which little significance was attached. The interview was therefore in a sense a strictly routine affair.

"Fennan's room at the Foreign Office was found to be unsuitable and we agreed to continue our discussion in St. James's Park, availing ourselves of the good weather.

"It has subsequently transpired that we were recognised and observed in this by an agent of the East German Intelligence Service, who had co-operated with me during the war. It is not certain whether he had placed Fennan under some kind of surveillance, or whether his presence in the park was coincidental.

"On the night of 3rd January it was reported by Surrey police that Fennan had committed suicide. A typewritten suicide note signed by Fennan claimed that he had been victimised by the security authorities.

"The following facts, however, emerged during investigation, and suggested foul play:

"1. At 7.55 P.M. on the night of his death Fennan had asked the Walliston exchange to call him at 8.30 the following morning.

"2. Fennan had made himself a cup of cocoa shortly before his death, and had not drunk it.

"3. He had supposedly shot himself in the hall, at the bottom of the stairs. The note was beside the body.

"4. It seemed inconsistent that he should type his last letter, as he seldom used a typewriter, and even more remarkable that he should come downstairs to the hall to shoot himself.

"5. On the day of his death he posted a letter inviting

139

me in urgent terms to lunch with him at Marlow the following day.

"6. Later it also transpired that Fennan had requested a day's leave for Wednesday, 4th January. He did not apparently mention this to his wife.

"7. It was also noted that the suicide letter had been typed on Fennan's own machine—and that it contained certain peculiarities in the typescript similar to those in the anonymous letter. The laboratory report concluded, however, that the two letters had not been typed by the same hand, though originating from the same machine.

"Mrs. Fennan, who had been to the theatre on the night her husband died, was invited to explain the 8.30 call from the exchange and falsely claimed to have requested it herself. The exchange was positive that this was not the case. Mrs. Fennan claimed that her husband had been nervous and depressed since his security interview, which corroborated the evidence of his final letter.

"On the afternoon of 4th January, having left Mrs. Fennan earlier in the day, I returned to my house in Kensington. Briefly observing somebody at the window, I rang the front-door bell. A man opened the door who has since been identified as a member of the East German Intelligence Service. He invited me into the house but I declined his offer and returned to my car, noting at the same time the numbers of cars parked nearby.

"That evening I visited a small garage in Battersea to enquire into the origin of one of these cars which was registered in the name of the proprietor of the garage. I was attacked by an unknown assailant and beaten senseless. Three weeks later the proprietor himself, Adam Scarr, was found dead in the Thames near Battersea Bridge. He had been drunk at the time of drowning. There were no signs of violence and he was known as a heavy drinker.

"It is relevant that Scarr had for the last four years provided an anonymous foreigner with the use of a car, and had received generous rewards for doing so. Their arrangements were designed to conceal the identity of the borrower even from Scarr himself, who only knew his client by the nickname 'Blondie' and could only reach him through a telephone number. The telephone number is of importance: it was that of the East German Steel Mission.

"Meanwhile, Mrs. Fennan's alibi for the evening of the murder had been investigated and significant information came to light:

"1. Mrs. Fennan attended the Weybridge Repertory Theatre twice a month, on the first and third Tuesdays. (*N.B.* Adam Scarr's client had collected his car on the first and third Tuesdays of each month.)

"2. She always brought a music case and left it in the cloakroom.

"3. When visiting the theatre she was always joined by a man whose description corresponded with that of my assailant and Scarr's client. It was even mistakenly assumed by a member of the theatre staff that this man was Mrs. Fennan's husband. He too brought a music case and left it in the cloakroom.

"4. On the evening of the murder Mrs. Fennan had left the theatre early after her friend had failed to arrive and had forgotten to reclaim her music case. Late that night she telephoned the theatre to ask if the case could be called for at once. She had lost her cloakroom ticket. The case was collected—by Mrs. Fennan's usual friend.

"At this point the stranger was identified as an employee of the East German Steel Mission named Mundt. The principal of the Mission was Herr Dieter Frey, a war-time collaborator of our Service, with extensive operational experience. After the war he had entered Government service in the Soviet zone of Germany. I should mention that Frey had operated with me during the war in enemy territory and had shown himself to be a brilliant and resourceful agent.

"I now decided to conduct a third interview with Mrs. Fennan. She broke down and confessed to having acted as an intelligence courier for her husband, who had been recruited by Frey on a skiing holiday five years ago. She herself had co-operated unwillingly, partly in loyalty to her husband and partly to protect him from his own carelessness in performing his espionage role. Frey had seen Fennan talking to me in the park. Assuming I was still operationally employed, he had concluded that Fennan was either under suspicion or a double agent. He instructed Mundt to liquidate Fennan, and his wife had been compelled into silence by her own complicity. She had even typed the text of the suicide letter on Fennan's typewriter over a specimen of her husband's signature.

"The means whereby she passed to Mundt the intelligence procured by her husband is relevant. She placed notes and copied documents in a music case, which she took to the theatre. Mundt brought a similar case containing money and instructions and, like Mrs. Fennan, left it in the cloakroom. They had only to exchange cloakroom tickets. When Mundt failed to appear at the theatre on the night in question, Mrs. Fennan obeyed standing instructions and posted the ticket to an address in Highgate. She left the theatre early in order to catch the last post from Weybridge. When later that night Mundt demanded the music case she told him what she had done. Mundt insisted on collecting the case that night, for he did not wish to make another journey to Weybridge.

"When I had interviewed Mrs. Fennan the following morning, one of my questions (about the 8.30 call) alarmed her so much that she telephoned Mundt. This accounts for the assault upon me later that day.

"Mrs. Fennan provided me with the address and telephone number she used when contacting Mundt—whom she knew by the cover name of Freitag. Both led to the apartment of a 'Lufteuropa' pilot who often entertained Mundt and provided accommodation for him when he required it. The pilot (presumably a courier of the East German Intelligence Service) has not returned to this country since 5th January.

"This, then, was the sum of Mrs. Fennan's revelations, and in a sense they led nowhere. The spy was dead, his murderers had vanished. It only remained to assess the extent of the damage. An official approach was now made to the Foreign Office and Mr. Felix Taverner was instructed to calculate from Foreign Office schedules what information had been compromised. This involved listing all files to which Fennan had had access since his recruitment by Frey. Remarkably, this revealed no systematic acquisition of secret files. Fennan had drawn no secret files except those which directly concerned him in his duties. During the last six months, when his access to sensitive papers was substantially increased, he had actually taken home *no* files of secret classification. The files he took home over this period were of universally low grade, and some treated subjects actually outside the scope of his section. This was not consistent with Fennan's role as a spy. It was, however, possible that he had lost heart for his work, and that his luncheon invitation to me was a first step to confession. With this in mind he might also have written the anonymous letter which could have been designed to put him in touch with the Department.

"Two further facts should be mentioned at this point. Under an assumed name and with a false passport, Mundt left the country by air on the day after Mrs. Fennan made her confession. He evaded the notice of the airport authorities, but was retrospectively identified by the air hostess. Secondly, Fennan's diary contained the full name and official telephone number of Dieter Frey—a flagrant breach of the most elementary rule of espionage.

"It was hard to understand why Mundt had waited three weeks in England after murdering Scarr, and even harder to reconcile Fennan's activities as described by his wife with the obviously unplanned and unproductive selection of files. Re-examination of the facts led repeatedly to this conclusion: the only evidence that Fennan was a spy came from his wife. If the facts were as she described them, why had she been allowed to survive the determination of Mundt and Frey to eliminate those in possession of dangerous knowledge?

"On the other hand, might she not herself be the spy?

143

"This would explain the date of Mundt's departure: he left as soon as he had been reassured by Mrs. Fennan that I had accepted her ingenious confession. It would explain the entry in Fennan's diary: Frey was a chance skiing acquaintance and an occasional visitor to Walliston. It would make sense of Fennan's choice of files—if Fennan deliberately chose unclassified papers at a time when his work was mainly secret there could be only one explanation: he had come to suspect his wife. Hence the invitation to Marlow, following naturally upon our encounter the previous day. Fennan had decided to tell me of his apprehensions and had taken a day's leave to do so—a fact of which his wife was not apparently aware. This would also explain why Fennan denounced himself in an anonymous letter: he wished to put himself in touch with us *as a preliminary to denouncing his wife.*

"Continuing the supposition it was remarkable that in matters of tradecraft Mrs. Fennan alone was efficient and conscientious. The technique used by herself and Mundt recalled that of Frey during the war. The secondary arrangement to post the cloakroom ticket if no meeting took place was typical of his scrupulous planning. Mrs. Fennan, it seemed, had acted with a precision scarcely compatible with her claim to be an unwilling party to her husband's treachery.

"While logically Mrs. Fennan now came under suspicion as a spy, there was no reason to believe that her account of what happened on the night of Fennan's murder was necessarily untrue. Had she known of Mundt's intention to murder her husband she would not have taken the music case to the theatre, and would not have posted the cloakroom ticket.

"There seemed no way of proving the case against her unless it was possible to reactivate the relationship between Mrs. Fennan and her controller. During the war Frey had devised an ingenious code for emergency communication by the use of snapshots and picture postcards. The actual subject of the photograph contained the message. A religious subject such as a painting of a Madonna or a church conveyed a request for an early meeting. The recipient would send in reply an entirely unrelated letter, making sure to date it. A meeting would take place at a prearranged time and place exactly five days after the date on the letter.

"It was just possible that Frey, whose tradecraft had evidently altered so little since the war, might have clung to this system—which, after all, would only seldom be needed. Relying on this I therefore posted to Elsa Fennan a picture postcard depicting a church. The card was posted from Highgate. I hoped somewhat forlornly that she would assume it had come to her through the agency of Frey. She reacted at once by sending to an unknown address abroad a ticket for a London theatre performance five days ahead. Mrs. Fennan's communication reached Frey, who accepted it as an *urgent summons*. Knowing that Mundt had been compromised by Mrs. Fennan's 'confession' he decided to come himself.

"They therefore met at the Sheridan Theatre, Hammersmith, on Thursday, 15th February.

"At first each assumed that the other had initiated the meeting, but when Frey realised they had been brought together by a deception he took drastic action. It may be that he suspected Mrs. Fennan of luring him into a trap, that he realised he was under surveillance. We shall never know. In any event, he murdered her. His method of doing this is best described in the coroner's report at the inquest: 'a single degree of pressure had been applied on the larynx, in particular to the horns of the thyroid cartilage, causing almost immediate death. It would appear that Mrs. Fennan's assailant was no layman in these matters.'

"Frey was pursued to a houseboat moored near Cheyne Walk, and while violently resisting arrest he fell into the river, from which his body has now been recovered."

XVIII

BETWEEN TWO WORLDS

Smiley's unrespectable club was usually empty on Sundays, but Mrs. Sturgeon left the door unlocked in case any of her gentlemen chose to call in. She adopted the same stern, possessive attitude towards her gentlemen as she had done in her landlady days at Oxford, when she had commanded from her fortunate boarders more respect than the entire assembly of dons and proctors. She forgave everything, but somehow managed to suggest on each occasion that her forgiveness was unique, and would never, never happen again. She had once made Steed-Asprey put ten shillings in the poor box for bringing seven guests without warning, and afterwards provided the dinner of a lifetime.

They sat at the same table as before. Mendel looked a shade sallower, a shade older. He scarcely spoke during the meal, handling his knife and fork with the same careful precision which he applied to any task. Guillam supplied most of the conversation, for Smiley, too, was less talkative than usual. They were at ease in their companionship and no one felt unduly the need to speak.

"Why did she do it?" Mendel asked suddenly.

Smiley shook his head slowly: "I think I know, but

we can only guess. I think she dreamed of a world without conflict, ordered and preserved by the new doctrine. I once angered her, you see, and she shouted at me: 'I'm the wandering Jewess,' she said; 'the no-man's land, the battlefield of your toy soldiers.' As she saw the new Germany rebuilt in the image of the old, saw the plump pride return, as she put it, I think it was just too much for her; I think she looked at the futility of her suffering and the prosperity of her persecutors and rebelled. Five years ago, she told me, they met Dieter on a skiing holiday in Germany. By that time the reestablishment of Germany as a prominent western power was well under way."

"Was she a communist?"

"I don't think she liked labels. I think she wanted to help build one society which could live without conflict. Peace is a dirty word now, isn't it? I think she wanted peace."

"And Dieter?" asked Guillam.

"God knows what Dieter wanted. Honour, I think, and a socialist world." Smiley shrugged. "They dreamed of peace and freedom. Now they're murderers and spies."

"Christ Almighty," said Mendel.

Smiley was silent again, looking into his glass. At last he said: "I can't expect you to understand. You only saw the end of Dieter. I saw the beginning. He went the full circle. I don't think he ever got over being a traitor in the war. He had to put it right. He was one of those world-builders who seem to do nothing but destroy: that's all."

Guillam gracefully intervened: "What about the 8.30 call?"

"I think it's pretty obvious. Fennan wanted to see me at Marlow and he'd taken a day's leave. He can't have told Elsa he was having a day off or she'd have tried to explain it away to me. He staged a phone call to give himself an excuse for going to Marlow. That's my guess, anyway."

The fire crackled in the wide hearth.

He caught the midnight plane to Zurich. It was a beautiful night, and through the small window beside him he watched the grey wing, motionless against the starlit sky, a glimpse of eternity between two worlds. The vision soothed him, calmed his fears and his doubts, made him fatalistic towards the inscrutable purpose of the universe. It all seemed to matter so little— the pathetic quest for love, or the return to solitude.

Soon the lights of the French coast came in sight. As he watched, he began to sense vicariously the static life beneath him; the rank smell of Gaulloises Bleues, garlic and good food, the raised voices in the bistro. Maston was a million miles off, locked away with his arid paper and his shiny politicians.

Smiley presented an odd figure to his fellow passengers—a little, fat man, rather gloomy, suddenly smiling, ordering a drink. The young, fair-haired man beside him examined him out of the corner of his eye. He knew the type well—the tired executive out for a bit of fun. He found it rather disgusting.

ABOUT THE AUTHOR

JOHN LE CARRÉ is the pseudonym of David Cornwell.
Born in 1931, he attended the universities of Berne and
Oxford, taught at Eton and later entered the British
Foreign Service. He has been described in *The New
York Times* as belonging to the select company of
such spy and detective story writers as Arthur Conan
Doyle, Dashiell Hammett, Raymond Chandler, and Ross
Macdonald. His first two novels were *Call for the Dead*
(1961) and *A Murder of Quality* (1962). His third novel,
The Spy Who Came in from the Cold (1963), was greet-
ed with great enthusiasm and secured his worldwide
reputation. Mr. le Carré is also the author of *The Naive
and Sentimental Lover, The Looking Glass War, A Small
Town in Germany, Tinker, Tailor, Soldier, Spy, The
Honourable Schoolboy, Smiley's People* and *The Little
Drummer Girl.*

JOHN LE CARRÉ

"The premier spy novelist of his time. Perhaps of all time," is what *Time* magazine recently called him.

Others echo the praise. But it took John le Carré many years to reach this position. He began his writing career while in the British Foreign Service. Unable to use his real name (David Cornwell) because the Foreign Office forbids its staff to publish under their own names, he adopted the name le Carré (French for "the square") which he claims to have seen printed on a London shop window.

As he states, "When I first began writing, Ian Fleming was riding high and the picture of the spy was that of a character who could have affairs with women, drive a fast car, who used gadgetry and gimmickry to escape." What le Carré has brought back is the realistic spy story.

Call for the Dead and *A Murder of Quality* were his first novels. It was his third novel *The Spy Who Came in from the Cold* which broke through to bestsellerdom. It features the antihero Alec Leamas, a cold war spy, out to rescue friends from Berlin. In *The Looking Glass War* our hero learns of the double-dealing needed to survive in the intelligence game. A change of pace, *A Naive and Sentimental Lover* follows an unhappy but successful businessman beguiled by a glamorous, wayward couple. *Tinker, Tailor, Soldier, Spy* followed. George Smiley (a minor character in *The Spy Who Came in from the Cold*) is the hero. Head of a British Intelligence department he must ferret out the "mole" who has wasted some of the department's best agents. Le Carré's bestseller *The Honourable Schoolboy* deals with Smiley's attempts to use one of his friends as a pawn to flush out a pair of mysterious Chinese brothers. *Smiley's People* chronicled Smiley's final confrontation with his greatest enemy, Karla. His latest #1 bestseller, *The Little Drummer Girl* will be published in paperback by Bantam in April 1984.

Le Carré, who has elevated the spy novel to its highest point, is a demon on research. For *The Honourable Schoolboy* he made five trips to Southeast Asia. Pinned down by automatic weapons fire in Cambodia, he dived under a car and coolly noted his impressions on file cards.

JOHN LE CARRÉ

' "Simply the world's greatest fictional spymaster."
—*Newsweek*

"Belongs in the select company of the best spy and detective writers. In all of his books, le Carré shows how endowed he is with the art of storytelling."
—*The Times* (London)

☐ **CALL FOR THE DEAD** (23172-3 • $3.50)
Le Carré's world-famous hero, George Smiley, is bitter and weary. He has seen too much and done too much—yet he cannot refuse one last desperate call for his services. Smiley returns to solve a baffling case involving a suspect British civil servant; a brilliant, twisted former hero of the German underground; a high-ranking pompous fool of a bureaucrat—and a once-beautiful woman with a terrifying secret.

☐ **A MURDER OF QUALITY** (23902-3 • $3.50)
Smiley emerges from retirement to solve a baffling, bloody crime. He becomes entangled with a woman as dangerous as she is charming . . . and a tottering, brilliant man haunted by a perverse secret from his past. Smiley pursues the murderer amid the hollow pomp and ceremony of the establishment, where a man's fate is decided over tea and a sentence of death can be passed out with biscuits and sherry . . .

☐ **THE SPY WHO CAME IN FROM THE COLD**
(23825-6 • $3.95)
With this superb novel of suspense, le Carré changed the rules of the game. His story is one last breathlessly perilous assignment for the agent who wants desperately to end his career of espionage—and "come in from the cold."

"The best spy story I have ever read."

—Graham Greene

☐ **THE LOOKING GLASS WAR (23693-8 • $3.95)**
Le Carré's hero in this powerful novel has a mission. He knows it is perilous. He has his orders: get your military intelligence any way you can. But it is a different kind of war and it calls for a different kind of fighting. The kind that is done quietly, in secret. It is the invisible war.

"A superb spy story."

—*Book Week*

☐ **THE NAIVE AND SENTIMENTAL LOVER**
   20989-2 • $3.95)
Le Carré's hero is Aldo Cassidy, "the naive and sentimental lover," a tycoon caught frantically between two astonishing loves. Trapped with him are Shamus, a wild artist who carouses by day or night, and Helen, the artist's nakedly alluring wife. Who will wind up with whom is only one of the mysteries in a world founded upon spontaneity and feeling . . .

"Sad, funny, captivating and stunningly fertile, it is the most satisfying novel I have read this year."

—*Sunday Express*

☐ **TINKER, TAILOR, SOLDIER, SPY**
   (22725-4 • $3.95)
Le Carré has created a remarkable challenge to Smiley and his people: a mole—a Soviet double agent—who's burrowed his way up to the highest level of British intelligence. His treachery has already blown some of their vital secret operations and their best networks. The mole is one of their own kind. But which one?

"One of the best tales of the year . . . A splendid assemblage of the virtues displayed in previous le Carré thrillers."

—*Time*

☐ **THE HONOURABLE SCHOOLBOY**
  (22791-2 • $3.95)

Smiley has become chief of the battered British Secret Service. The betrayal of a Soviet double agent has riddled the spy network. Smiley wants revenge. He chooses his weapon: "The Honourable Schoolboy," Jerry Westerby, a passionate lover and a reckless, seasoned secret agent. He points him east to Hong Kong. So begins the terrifying game . . .

"John le Carré is the premier spy novelist of his time. Perhaps of all time."

—*Time*

☐ **SMILEY'S PEOPLE** (23149-9 • $3.95)

Here le Carré gives us the last chapter—the final agonizing confrontation—between George Smiley and Karla, his mortal enemy and opposite number inside the Soviet Union.

"The ultimate espionage novel."

—*Publishers Weekly*

Read all of John le Carré's remarkable novels, on sale now wherever Bantam paperbacks are sold, or use the handy coupon below for ordering:

THE REMARKABLE #1 BESTSELLER
NOW IN PAPERBACK

JOHN LE CARRÉ

THE LITTLE DRUMMER GIRL

Here is the terrifying adventure of Charlie, a young actress forced to play the ultimate role in the secret pursuit of a dangerous and elusive terrorist leader. This is John le Carré's richest and most thrilling novel yet, plunging us into entirely new labyrinths of intrigue, into the dark heart of modern-day terrorism.

"A TRIUMPH." —*Time*

"AN IRRESISTIBLE BOOK ... CHARLIE IS THE ULTIMATE DOUBLE AGENT." —*The New York Times*

Buy THE LITTLE DRUMMER GIRL, on sale April 1, 1984, wherever Bantam paperbacks are sold.

LeCarré-1